EVE'S LONGING
The Infinite Possibilities In All Things

EVE'S LONGING

The Infinite Possibilities In All Things

BY DEBORAH MCKAY

FICTION COLLECTIVE TWO

Boulder • Normal

Published by Illinois State University and Fiction Collective Two
with support given by the IllinoisState University Fine Arts Festival,
the Illinois State University President's Discretionary Fund, the
English Department Publications Unit of Illinois State University,
the English Department Publications Center of the University of
Colorado at Boulder, the Illinois Arts Council, and the National
Endowment for the Arts

Address all inquiries to: Fiction Collective Two, ℅ English Department, Publications Center, University of Colorado at Boulder,
Boulder, Colorado 80309-0494

Eve's Longing: The Infinite Possibilities In All Things
Deborah McKay

ISBN: Cloth, 0-932511-64-3
ISBN: Paper, 0-932511-65-1

Produced and printed in the United States of America
Distributed by the Talman Company

Book and Cover Design: Jean C. Lee

This book is dedicated
with a love and gratitude
beyond all words
to

my father,

ARTHUR R. MCKAY
1918-1989

my soul mate,

STEVEN A. KRAFT
1951-1990

and my dear friend,

KAREN A. BRINER
1945 -1966

CONTENTS

My love and deepest gratitude goes to

Cummington Community of the Arts, which made it possible for me to live and work in its beautiful environment with my daughter and be both a full-time writer and a full-time mother,

The Lawrenceville School, which has continued for many years to support and encourage me in my writing and in so many other ways,

Denise Levertov, James Hillman, and William Wise, who helped me so very generously in the editing of the book,

Michael Stephens, who encouraged and aided me in sending the book out,

Carole Maso, who was the book's tireless and faithful midwife during an extraordinarily long and painful birthing process and without whom I may well have given up,

And especially to my daughter, Milana, my love for whom was the primary thing that kept me from becoming Eve.

He who has seen the whole world hanging on a hair of the mercy of God has seen the truth; we might almost say the cold truth. He who has seen the vision of his city upside-down has seen it right way up.

ST. FRANCIS OF ASSISI
G. K. Chesterton

PART ONE

New York City

Chapter One

Eve opens her eyes and sits up in bed, clutching the bed sheets up around her neck with one hand, while she leans over and opens the window with the other hand. She grabs the birds, one by one, from the window ledge and stuffs them into the wide-mouthed jar on her bedside table, poking them down into the jar with the eraser end of a pencil.

"Get in there, you little brats!" she snaps at them as she jabs their round heads with her pencil, packing them down tightly, while still clutching the sheets up around her neck.

By the time she has filled the jar to the brim, she is out of breath, yet she manages to screw the metal lid on and then pound it down with her fist, until her hand aches and the lid is tight.

Now that there is no chance of the birds escaping, she leans back on her pillows and takes a deep breath. She keeps her eyes fixed on the glass jar, watching the birds trying to move within its confines.

They are squirming around in the jar, trying to breathe, but Eve has figured out that she has packed them so tightly that they are now limited to two possibilities:

1. They can move, and risk injuring one another, or
2. They can not move.

She herself was reduced to the same, two possibilities a week ago, and had chosen to remain motionless in bed.

The birds, on the other hand, decide to move, and, therefore, the wing of one of them pierces a hole in the stomach of another, their feathers knot and tangle, until they begin to become indistinguishable from one another, and then, finally, it is impossible to tell where one bird ends and the next begins. Their movement has woven them together, glued wing-on-wing by their own white paste. They are smashed up against the jar in pleached patterns.

Eve waits until their motion has ceased altogether, and then she reaches one hand down into the jar. She pulls out the contents, which, to her delight, have been woven into one, large, pasty bird-shawl. She releases the bed sheets from her grip and wraps the shawl about her shoulders. The room fills with the smell of dead sparrows.

The shawl is lovely: the way three bird's eyes have been glued down the front like shiny buttons, with talons creating a delicate embroidery along the edges. Eve relaxes back into her pillows, snuggling in the shawl.

Her brief moment of peace is interrupted by an overwhelming desire to analyze the birds, to figure them out, to arrive at a theory as to their ontological status. But the scraping she hears out in the hallway is even more compelling.

She presumes there are more birds out in the hallway, pecking at the faded, yellow-flowered wallpaper. She listens attentively. Yes, she can distinctly hear more birds out there, although the door to the hall is closed, so she can't see them. She hears them beckoning to her.

"Get up, you bum!" they whisper to her through the keyhole of the door. They are breathing *her* air and eating *her* wallpaper and yet have the nerve to hurl insults and challenges at her!

"Planning to sleep for another week, you slut?" they ask her, in snide tones, through the crack of the door.

Finally, she pushes herself up from the bed, neatly buttons the shawl down the front, and opens the door to the hallway. Her legs are weak from lying in bed for so long. They buckle and she lurches forward, catching herself with her hand on the opposite wall. She feels something slippery, lifts her hand and finds a detached wing, greasy as if buttered. It sticks to the palm of her hand, and she tries to shake it off, but it clings. She pries it off with her foot, but then it sticks to her foot, so she has to hop on the other foot down the hallway, toward the kitchen.

The hall is filled now with birds, sickly specimens, unhealthy, city birds, ramming against the walls in aborted flight, thudding onto her back, dead weights, feathers up her nose, a talon holding one of her eyes shut, wings scraping across her, opening little, bleeding slits in her skin.

But she persists in making her way, slowly, down the hall, hopping, stumbling, and, finally, crawling. She is sweating under the shawl, making her way toward the kitchen, inch by inch. Then, suddenly, she bursts out laughing. She gets up on her knees and grabs one of the birds in mid-flight, holds it tightly in both hands and kisses it smack on the top of its head. Then she tosses it up into the air again.

"Get the hell out of here!" she yells at all of them. She is actually beginning to feel grateful they have come, since this is motion after a week's damp stillness. Their wings have smacked her awake.

Chapter Two

It has taken Eve over half an hour to get down the hallway from her bedroom to the kitchen. Even after the birds had finally flown off, it still took her fifteen more minutes to crawl on her hands and knees, over slippery mounds of feathers, until she made it into the kitchen.

Now she pulls herself up into a chair at the kitchen table and looks around the room. An acidic taste rises in her throat, but she swallows it back down. She makes a decision to do something appropriate. But it's hard to think straight, with these bird feathers sticking out from her nightgown pocket, a few stuck in her hair, two glued to her legs. But she is determined, closes her eyes, takes a deep breath, and forces herself to concentrate. She formulates the basic question:

"What would be the appropriate behavior of a woman sitting at her kitchen table?" she queries.

Of course, as is true in all philosophical inquiry, once the question has been formulated, the answer follows easily. Clearly, one, appropriate act would be to eat something.

So Eve begins to look for something to eat. She notices, for the first time in a week, that she is hungry. She can't recall eating at all during the week she has been in bed. Yes, she is beginning to feel quite hungry now. In fact, she can't remember ever being this hungry before.

After searching through the refrigerator and all the cupboards, she has finally arrived at the perfect thing. It is a can of baby peas. She realizes, with a surge of joy, that if she could chose *anything* in the universe at this moment to eat, it would be this very can of peas.

She takes the can and carefully opens it, so as not to spill any of the juice, and pours the whole can into a bowl in front of her. Without a doubt, she has never in her life seen a more delicious meal before her. How delicately the color of the peas is echoed by that of their pale green juice! Her mouth waters for the peas and the liquid bathing them so tenderly.

She sits staring at the bowl with growing appetite, but nothing else happens. There seems to be some problem, something causing the chain of events to have halted.

"What happens next?" she questions.

She states the problem out loud:

"Number One: I am hungry.

Number Two: There is something wonderful to eat in front of me.

And Number Three: I do not seem to be eating."

It should be so simple, she thinks to herself. She recalls having eaten nearly every day of her life, and yet this morning she seems to have lost the knack.

She decides to further assess the situation and define the problem. She thinks for a moment in silent meditation. Ah! she has it. She needs a way of getting the peas up from the bowl and into her mouth. She needs a *means of transportation* for the peas. She is determined to figure this out.

"The first element," she reasons to herself, "we shall call 'A' (my mouth), desperately needs a direct way of relating to the second element, call it 'B' (the peas). Clearly, the middle link is missing. There needs to be an overall design, in which both 'A' and 'B' can function mutually together. Perhaps if I made a diagram of this? I used to be able to solve these problems so easily."

Eve has been sitting in front of the peas now for forty-five minutes, growing increasingly frantic, conceptualizing every possible solution for how one might relate A to B, and yet she has not tasted so much as a *single pea*! Her eyes keep darting about the room, looking for a clue. She is trying to be patient, trying to be calm and reasonable, trying to recollect how she has done this in the past.

Then, finally (as if not by her own reason, but by divine inspiration) she discovers the missing link: the *spoon*! She leaps up from the chair, snatches a large soup spoon from the dish drainer, and scoops the peas into her mouth. In her haste, some of the juice sloshes over the edge of the spoon and slides down over her wrist and then on down her arm. After she has finished every pea, she lifts the bowl in both hands and pours the rest of the juice into her mouth and then licks the bowl clean.

Chapter Three

After licking the bowl clean, Eve looks up to see spinning grey wings encircling her head. She feels dizzy, closes her eyes and puts her head down on the kitchen table and falls asleep. A few minutes later, Eve's sister, Clare, with whom Eve shares the apartment, arrives home, carefully balancing three full bags of groceries and a bouquet of white carnations in her arms. Clare smiles with pleasure, at seeing Eve up out of bed. There have been times when Eve's retreats to bed have lasted far longer than this one.

Clare tiptoes over and puts one of the bags of groceries down in the sink, one in the dish drainer and one in the other chair at the table, so as not to disturb Eve. Then she goes over to Eve and feels her forehead. It feels normal. Clare quietly puts away all the groceries, goes into Eve's bedroom and changes her sheets and closes the open window. Then she goes back into the kitchen and gently strokes Eve's head.

Eve blinks and looks up at Clare, still not quite awake.

"You're up!" Clare says cheerily.

Eve makes no response. She just stares around the room, blinking, with a puzzled expression, as if she didn't know where she was.

"I'm so glad you're up because Dad's in town," says Clare. "He was hoping you could join him for lunch today. I can't come because I have to work the lunch shift."

Eve nods her head without saying anything.

"You probably should start getting ready if you want to go," says Clare. "You'd have to leave in about an hour."

Eve bolts upright in her chair and gasps. "In an *hour*?" she says in disbelief. "I'll never make it!" She looks at Clare, her face panic-striken.

"Yes, you will," says Clare. "I'll run a bath for you." She takes Eve's hand and leads her into the bathroom.

After Clare goes back into the kitchen, Eve shuts the bathroom door and locks it. Then she turns off the cold water and fills the rest of the tub with just hot water. Her hands are trembling so badly she can hardly undo the buttons on the bird shawl. The shawl is slippery and slides out of her hands and falls into the bathtub. A stain emerges from it in the hot water. Eve reaches in and pulls it out, scalding her hands. She wrings the shawl out in the sink, wraps it in a huge bath towel, drains the tub, scrubs it out with Ajax, puts in more hot water and finally climbs in.

The submerged part of her body aches and turns bright red, but she hardly notices. She scrubs herself very hard with a rough sponge and lots of soap, beginning at the top of her forehead and moving down her body systematically, so as not to miss a single spot, concentrating especially on her arm where the pea juice has hardened. Then she washes her hair, scrubbing her scalp vigorously, in little circular motions, digging her nails in, rinsing and shampooing over and over. Then she lets the water out of the tub, but the drain is clogged with feathers. She frantically pulls the feathers out and flushes them down the toilet.

She turns on the shower and stands up. She takes a clean wash-cloth and repeats the previous process, in exactly the same sequence, but with a different soap and shampoo. She stands for a long time letting the water pound on her head. Then she gets out and dries herself carefully with six different towels and brushes her teeth for twenty minutes, using up the toothpaste four times and adding more, spitting out blood where she brushes too hard on her gums.

She looks at herself in the floor-length mirror, sees a hair on her breast, so she turns on the shower again, gets back in and rinses the hair off, this time checking to make sure all hairs, pea juice and feathers have been removed before getting out. Then she sits on the edge of the tub and clips her fingernails and toenails into the tub.

As she washes the nail clippings down the drain, she remembers one time when she and Clare were on their way to meet their father for dinner. Just as Eve was putting a token into the slot at the subway station, she found herself paralyzed and knew something was drastically wrong with her fingers holding the token. She looked down at them and noticed that she had neglected to clip her fingernails. So she had grabbed Clare's arm and made her come back up into the street with her and wait while she ran into a drugstore, bought a pair of nail clippers, and clipped her nails carefully over a trashbasket.

Eve is staring at the water swirling in a spiral down the bathtub drain. She feels a chill come over her body and sees a tiny image of her father spinning in the water. He is only the length and width of her thumb and is wearing a neatly pressed, grey summer suit, a perfectly starched white shirt and a navy blue tie with very tiny white dots on it. She stares at the white dots, thinking about how evenly spaced they are on his tie. She hates those dots and reaches down to pry them off with one of her fingernail clippings, but too late, he has swirled down the drain.

Now she pictures her father looking at her across the table in the restaurant. She can smell his wonderful, freshly-starched shirt and his after shave, Aqua Velva. She wants to put her head on his shoulder to rest, to smell him better. She leaps up and looks in the bathroom mirror. She pulls her long, wet hair back into a tight rubberband, smoothing every strand of hair down flat against her head. Then she sprays deodorant on, waits for it to dry, and sprays it on again, three times.

Clare knocks tentatively on the door. "You better get dressed," she suggests. Eve desperately wants to take another quick shower, but she resists, and goes into her room to get dressed. Clare has laid out some fresh clothes for her on the bed. Eve changes her blouse four times and her skirt twice. Nothing looks right. She grabs more clothes from the closet, even winter clothes, although it is mid-August. There is something wrong with everything she puts on: broken zippers, missing buttons, rips and stains. Clare comes to the door of Eve's bedroom.

"You look fine," she says encouragingly. "You just buttoned it wrong." She unbuttons Eve's blouse and re-does it. Then she hands Eve her purse and a piece of paper with the name and address of the restaurant where Eve is to meet her father. Then she leads Eve to the front door. Eve sighs and reluctantly hurries uptown to meet her father.

Chapter Four

Eve approaches her father as she always does, stumbling toward him, heart trembling, blood rushing to her head, not seeing anything on the street, but, instead, imagining herself waving enormous palm fronds and bowing before him. She imagines she has burnt offerings for him in her purse, in a small bag made of red velvet: chunks of whole frankincense and myrrh. She trips on the curb, catches herself on one knee, tears her stocking, jumps back up and runs on, afraid to be late.

As she hurries toward him, though he is still sixty blocks uptown, she begins chanting to herself, as she often does, chanting a passage from some philosopher or theologian in her head, repeating it over and over again, like a mantra. She must keep it in her head so that it is ready, should she need to toss it out as a barrier between them. Today the passage that has popped into her head is from Wittgenstein:

> *Whereof one cannot speak, thereof one must be silent.*
> *Whereof one cannot speak, thereof one must be silent.*

She says it over and over while she waits impatiently for the subway, tapping her foot to the rhythm of the words.

> *Whereof one cannot speak, thereof one must be silent.*
> *Whereof one cannot speak, thereof one must be silent.*

She is afraid, as always, that her father will find out that she doesn't understand this passage, so she tries another.

Cogito ergo sum.
Cogito ergo sum.
Cogito ergo sum.

But after saying it three times, the words start sounding strange and she can't remember what they mean. They stick in her throat like a lump of phlegm. She gags. She can't remember what it means! She tries chanting another phrase, this time very slowly. In fact, she is chanting it so slowly, it sounds like a record on the wrong speed:

To be is to be perceived.
To be is to be perceived.

But this phrase sounds all wrong too. She wonders if it is backwards and tries it the other way around: "To be perceived is to be"? She pictures her father looking at her in disappointment. She knows full well that he's always been the brilliant theologian and she his clumsy apprentice, unable to handle even the most elementary philosophical truths (although she always pretends to understand them perfectly). The best she can hope for is that at least he won't find out *today* that she knows nothing. She will agree with him and nod her head, as always, and pray, her hands clasped under the table, that he won't ask her any questions she can't answer.

When Eve gets out of the subway, the heel of her sandal gets caught on a grate and rips off. She bends over and picks it up, puts it back in place and stamps her foot furiously. She wonders if perhaps she should run into a store and buy some glue to glue it back on, but she is afraid of being late. What to do? What if the heel should fall off as they walk to the table in the restaurant? She couldn't bear it. Well, the heel seems to be staying on for the time being, and with each step she stamps down hard on it, limping along the sidewalk like a cripple, hoping the little nails will hold it on, even without the proper glue.

When Eve arrives at the restaurant, her father is waiting just inside the door. They give each other a quick hug and sit down at the table he has reserved. They make a handsome pair, both very tall and thin, with a striking resemblance to each other, especially in the forehead, cheekbones and nose, clearly father and daughter. He looks distinguished as always, in his grey suit, his navy blue tie with the white dots on it, and, of course, his slim leather briefcase under his arm. Even Eve looks respectable, wearing a tailored, white blouse with tucks in the front and a grey, pleated skirt. No one would suspect from her appearance that the hem of her skirt is unsewn and is being held up by a piece of masking tape.

As is their habit, they leap headlong into a shared catechism, which they recite each time they are alone together and are forced to make conversation. The catechism consists of questions and answers concerning various members of the family and anything else safely benign. This catechism has as its essential property the fact that its questions will never delve beyond the level of harmless inquiry. The catechism circles over the same material in increasing detail, like a spiral, until the time has been filled and they are allowed to stop. That tedious spiralling pushes her shoulders over into their habitual slump, humping her back out, her head hanging over her plate as if in prayer. She succeeds in mumbling appropriate responses until, at the last minute, just as their time together is almost up, Eve surprises both of them by blurting out,

"Dad, what do you think of Anselm's ontological proof?"

For a split second just after she asks the question, she imagines her question leaping out from her mouth and wrapping around her father like an arm, drawing him closer to her, drawing them into an intimate embrace of words, a sharing of their heartfelt secrets: him confessing those hidden thoughts he has never told to anyone, confessing how special she is to him, his first-born, the apple of his eye; and she confessing to him how beautiful and perfect he is to her, how desperately she has always wanted to be exactly like him, how much she wants him to approve of her, to think she's smart, how much she wants to be his confidant, how much she loves the smell of his Aqua Velva.

Suddenly she remembers the question she has just asked him and looks up at him.

"Anselm was definitely on the right track," he says, "despite the fact that his argument is obviously tautological".

His face looks as it so often does to her, when she has the courage to look at him directly, as if he were braced against some secret pain, as if there were dozens of straight pins sticking into him, one under each dot in his tie.

"And what do *you* think of the proof?" he asks her, always turning the question back on her as soon as he can, like all good Socratics.

She sighs. "You're right," she says, wanting to continue the conversation, but too afraid that her words will rush out like spurts of blood or spit, staining his tie. She just shrugs her shoulders and smiles awkwardly at him. As she smiles, she notices that the left side of her mouth is higher than the right, so she coughs as an excuse to cover her crooked mouth. Her father hands her his handkerchief, as she knew he would. She breathes in his familiar smell and secretly wipes away a few tears while he studies the check.

They wait in endless, painful silence, while the waitress takes her father's credit card and comes back. Finally, they go out into the street and he hails her a cab. They exchange safe, *pro forma* hugs and she hastily leaps into the cab. The heel of her sandal drops into the gutter as the door slams, but neither of them notices.

Chapter Five

Eve tries hard not to vomit in the cab. Her head is spinning as the cab weaves violently through the city traffic. The cab smells like urine and pizza, and her body is weak with vertigo, so she falls off the seat and lands, ungracefully, on one knee on the filthy floor. She reaches down to remove a Snicker's wrapper stuck to her knee and it is then that she notices that the heel of her sandal is gone. She gasps as she imagines her father bending down to pick up the heel as her cab had sped away. What a *fool* she is!

When she gets back to her apartment, she tears off her clothes and jumps in bed, her head throbbing. But the spinning gets worse when she lies down, so she goes into the bathroom and makes herself vomit in the toilet, thinking how her father wasted his money on that elegant luncheon, flushed away weeks before Mastercard would send him the bill. Then she gets back in bed. Clare has left for work and there is no one to talk to, so she tries to sleep.

She buries her head in the pillow, trying to conjure the smell of Aqua Velva. Images are spinning round her: she sees her father holding her head in his hand, moments after she was born. His favorite story to tell her has always been how when she was born, she was so small, that he could lay her head in his hand and her feet only reached to the crook of his arm. Then she sees her father holding the heel of her sandal in his hand, but it looks more like a wafer he has just blessed and holds out to her to take for communion. Then she sees herself as a small child, sitting between her mother and Clare, in the front pew of the church where her father was the pastor, before he had become a seminary president. She is staring up at him in his wonderful, long, black velvet robe, his hand held out over the congregation in benediction. His head is glowing, his hand outstretched to her, offering her the little round wafer.

How she had strained as a child to understand his sermons, and later, his lectures at the seminary, taking endless notes, believing with all her heart that the key to everything was in her father's words, in his world of philosophical theology, the world of ontological proofs for the existence of God, if she could just grasp it.

Eve dozes off now, dreaming of her father preaching from a little blue rowboat, off the shore in front of their summer cottage.

Her mother had taught gym at the private school she and Clare had attended. Eve had made a solemn vow to herself that she would despise all forms of physical exercise and openly deride people who showed the slightest interest in sports. Her mother was often humiliated by Eve at school, when Eve would refuse to participate in her mother's gym classes and her mother had to send Eve to the principal.

One day, when Eve was in the eighth grade, she had pretended to have cramps and had been allowed to sit out on the sidelines. She was sitting on a bench, absorbed in reading Plato's *Republic* for the third time. Her mother called to her and asked her to hold the long rope hanging from the ceiling while she showed some girls in the class how to shinny up it. Her mother never gave up trying to drag Eve into the physical world. Every day after school, when Clare and her mother went to field hockey practice, Eve would rush back to the seminary just in time to attend her father's class on Systematic Theology. Eve prided herself on being totally out of shape and joked about not wanting any more muscles in her body than were absolutely necessary to enable her to turn a page in *The Republic*.

When Eve pretended not to hear her mother's request to hold the rope for her, her mother asked another girl in the gym class to do it. Eve peered over her book for a second to watch her mother climbing up the rope toward the ceiling. Despite being slightly overweight, her mother was very strong and agile. As she got almost to the top, the girl holding the rope at the bottom was suddenly knocked off her feet by a basketball careening through the air from the other end of the gym. The rope was jerked out of the girl's hand and spun out into the air. Up near the ceiling, Eve's mother lost her balance and began to fall. She grasped for the rope as she fell, but she and the rope were spinning away from each other in opposite directions and she couldn't regain her grip.

The Republic dropped out of Eve's hands with a thud when her mother hit the ground. All the girls began screaming and looking over at Eve. But Eve was paralyzed. She couldn't get up to go over to her mother, who lay perfectly still on the floor of the gym.

When the ambulance arrived, her mother was already dead. She had died the moment she hit the floor. There was no blood, and no external sign of injury. As they carried her mother out on the stretcher, Eve noticed she looked like she was sleeping. Eve reached down and picked up The Republic. The school nurse came over and led Eve out of the gym. Eve kept one finger in The Republic so as not to lose her place.

Chapter Six

Two hours later, Eve wakes with a jolt and realizes she had fallen asleep and has had many dreams, the last of which is still going on. She is in her spiral dream, her whole body still spinning round and round the circles of the spiral. She clutches the headboard, trying to steady herself. She shakes her head back and forth, smacks her face a few times quite hard, and squeezes her eyes open and shut, until the spinning slows down. She weaves unsteadily out of bed, gets one of her many, large black drawing books, and takes it back to bed with her. She begins drawing the spiral in her book, from different angles.

This same exact dream of the spiral has recurred for as long as Eve can remember. She can even recall seeing the spiral caught in the bars of her crib one night, when she was a baby.

In this dream, Eve is trapped inside a huge spiral, which is inside a cone, being spun around in circles, starting where it is widest, at the top, and being pushed round and round, down toward the tip at the bottom. She makes arrows on her drawing, showing the direction of her movement within the spiral, hoping the act of drawing will make the dream stop.

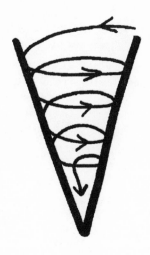

Every time she has this dream, Eve gets more terrified of hitting the bottom and tenses all her muscles against it. But no matter how much she resists, she is pushed a little farther down the spiral each time. Luckily, so far she has never hit the bottom.

As a child, Eve had developed ways of trying to make the dream stop. She would even force herself to stay awake all night if she sensed that she might have the dream. She would go into the bathroom every few minutes and drench her head under the cold water in the tub. If she awoke in the middle of the dream, she would open her bedroom window wide and suck in the night air, quickly, in huge gulps, and then she would make tiny, hard pinches in her cheeks and her eyelids with her fingernails.

Most nightmares that lingered upon waking, when she was a child, could be finally dispelled by Eve's getting in bed between her parents. But not this one—it only got worse, so she stayed in her room alone and tried to invent new ways to make it stop.

As she is drawing, Eve is suddenly shocked to notice that there are very long, narrow spirals running the length of each of her finger-nails! She studies the fingernails on her left hand intensely, while quickly making a few sketches of these newfound spirals in her drawing book.

The spirals seem to originate under the moon of her cuticle and spin up to where they have been cut off at the upper edges of her fingernails. She notices that on one finger there is a little cut in the skin, just at the point where the spiral disappears under the skin. She pries that slit open further, with the tip of her pen, and then, finding the pen inadequate, she tears the skin open still further with a pair of tweezers. Her whole finger throbs, but she is anxious to know whether the spiral can be seen to continue underneath the skin. Unfortunately, her finger begins bleeding and the spiral, if it is there, is invisible in the blood.

"Cut off at the top of the nail, and lost in blood at the bottom," she says to herself. "Lost in both *ascent* and *descent*," she summarizes.

She suddenly puts down the drawings, jumps up from bed, and walks deliberately through the kitchen, out the back door of the apartment, and down the back service stairs. She reaches the bottom of the first flight of stairs, leans over the edge of the bottom step, balances, holding the railing and looking for the next step and the landing between flights. But she sees nothing except empty space. So she turns around and heads back up the stairs. But here, at the top of the flight, is also empty space. So she turns around and goes back down again, retracing her steps, going faster now. At the bottom step, she again peers over the edge as far as she can see. It is still just empty space, no stairs in sight. So she turns and climbs back up to the top again, running now, straining up into the empty space at the top, but seeing nothing, beginning to panic, then going back down again to the bottom, two steps at a time, and then up again, down again, reversing her direction each time she reaches empty space. Suddenly it occurs to her that the spirals of her fingernails have somehow been magnified a thousand times, and she is running up and down within them.

A delivery boy, carrying a case of beer, passes her on the stairs, finds the landing, turns and ascends another flight invisible to Eve. She hurries back into the apartment, and, holding each hand up to the light, carefully copies the spirals and slits on each finger, each in its own, separate diagram, being sure to include specks of dirt, blood and waves of cuticle.

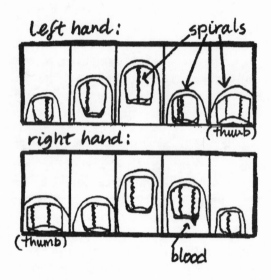

She labels each drawing and dates it. Then she covers her hands by putting on a pair of old, white cotton gloves her mother had given her to wear to church when she was in fifth grade. The fingertip of one glove slowly turns bright red.

Chapter Seven

$\mathbf{J}$ust as Eve labels the last fingernail diagram, Clare comes in the door. Eve jumps up and runs to meet her.

"I need to talk to you," says Eve. "I have to tell you about The Pearl String."

"Going to Sunday School?" asks Clare, looking at Eve's white gloves.

"I need to talk to you about The Pearl String. Please!" begs Eve.

"How about tomorrow morning?" asks Clare. "I'm really tired."

"I can't wait until tomorrow," says Eve. "I've been waiting all day to talk to you. It won't take long. Please? I'll make some coffee while you change. O.K.?"

"All right," says Clare, reluctantly, with a deep sigh.

Eve claps her white-gloved hands together and rushes into the kitchen. She waits only until the water has heated to lukewarm, hurriedly makes the coffee, and then rushes into her bedroom to get some notebooks.

Clare goes into the bathroom and washes her face, takes some aspirin, and changes into her bathrobe. Then she joins Eve, who is sitting on the couch in the living room, with one of her large, black drawing books open beside her.

"O.K., I'm ready," says Clare, attempting a cheerful tone. Clare has heard Eve mention "The Pearl String" in the midst of various conversations, but Eve has never explained what it was. Clare hands

Eve a cup of coffee. She has already put in the cream and sugar and stirred it for her. Eve holds the coffee cup in both hands. A shudder runs up her back and she spills some coffee on her leg. She doesn't notice. Clare wipes Eve's leg with a napkin and lays it over her lap. She is hoping it's not going to be one of those long nights listening to one of Eve's complicated theories—she doesn't really feel up to it.

"Here's a drawing of The Pearl String," Eve says, enthusiastically, handing Clare the opened drawing book and pointing to a diagram.

"The Pearl String is simply a piece of white, cotton string on which are strung white pearls," she says, pointing to the drawing.

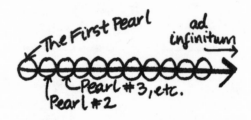

"This string of pearls stretches out in a horizontal line, a line which goes out to the right infinitely," she says, pointing.

Clare looks at the drawing for a minute and then says, "So far so good." She has tasted the coffee by now and has realized it is lukewarm and puts her cup down, disappointed.

"Each of these pearls represents a particular mode of existence," continues Eve, "and there are an infinite number of possible modes." She points to each pearl in the drawing as she talks. "The First Pearl, so labeled," she says, pointing to the first pearl on the left of the string, "is the mode of ordinary reality: normal, everyday existence, like we're in now. In fact, this is where we all reside almost all the time. Most people have never left this first pearl. In the First Pearl, things operate according to ordinary rules and logic, like the law of gravity. This makes most things very predictable and reliable. For example, if you're in this First Pearl, and you drop a cat out the window," (she points to the window as a reference point) "you can predict with assurance that the cat will fall *down*, not up." She looks up at Clare. Clare nods and says, "Down, not up."

"Or, for another example, in this First Pearl, if you get into a bathtub full of water, you will get wet, or if you add one and one, you will get two. Here in the First Pearl, people make agreements and can make safe assumptions. The biggest agreement, of course, is language, we agree on what words mean. Like if I say, 'Pass me the salt,' I can safely assume that we are agreed on what that means, so I can assume you will understand me, and, therefore, will pass me the salt." She looks at Clare for confirmation.

"Like if I say, 'Would you like more coffee', you say?" asks Clare.

"What?" asks Eve.

"Would you like more coffee?"

"Would you like more coffee? Oh. Right. Yeah that's what I mean."

"Well, would you like more coffee?"

"Oh. No. No, thanks. You see, the First Pearl is the finite world. One of our biggest assumptions here is that everything eventually dies." She pauses for a moment, thinking. "The hardest part is to get *out* of that First Pearl and into the next one, and then the next, into these other modes of existence."

"Yes," says Clare. "I have found it hard *not* to be finite." Eve doesn't seem to have heard this and continues.

"Most people never even guess that leaving the First Pearl is a *possibility*. And those who do know it's possible, spend most of their lives forgetting that it is, and when they do remember, it is almost impossible to do. You don't just say to yourself, 'Today I will leave the First Pearl behind.' It doesn't happen that easily."

"No, I suppose not," says Clare.

"And most people are too afraid to leave the First Pearl, afraid of not getting back to the First Pearl, afraid of being without those safe rules and that predictability."

"Yes," nods Clare. "It frightens some people when cats start falling up." Eve continues talking.

"If you do manage to get *out* of the First Pearl, you can proceed on to the other pearls along the string much more easily. It's getting out of that First Pearl that's so hard."

"Sounds like a killer," says Clare.

"In fact," Eve continues, " once you get out of that First Pearl, there is a compelling force moving you along from one pearl to the next, a force that accelerates as you move farther away from the First Pearl. It's hard for us to imagine what it's like out there, now, while we're here in the First Pearl. I've walked out along The Pearl String so many times, and yet, as I'm sitting here talking to you, I can't really remember what it was like. I only have words to describe it: symbols for that experience, not the experience itself. I just know that the farther you get away from the First Pearl, the more pure your experiences become, because, of course, your experiences aren't obscured by judgements, analyses, logic, rationality, by the filter of language." She pauses, a frown come over her face, thinking to herself.

"So, if you throw a cat out the window in Pearl Two or Three, what happens?" asks Clare. Eve, preoccupied with her own thoughts does not answer but keeps talking.

"Sometimes I start feeling light-headed and dizzy and my head starts reeling, as if I had been twirling in circles, and then, suddenly, I see The Pearl String in front of me: those beautiful, clean, white pearls, waiting for me, just sitting there waiting, like birds on a wire."

"Birds on a wire," repeats Clare.

"I always feel so *relieved* when I see The Pearl String and remember the possibility of leaving this dull First Pearl behind, of spitting it out like a fat pea and taking another pearl in my mouth, rolling it on my tongue for a while, until I get its full taste, and then tasting the next pearl, and the next, one after another, holding them on my tongue, savoring them until they become as familiar as my own saliva."

Clare has been keeping an eye on the cup of coffee Eve is holding, which keeps tilting more and more and is about to spill. Clare knows it would stain the white couch, so she gently takes the cup from Eve and places it on the coffee table. Eve doesn't notice and keeps on talking, a frightened look now appearing in her face.

"Sometimes when I'm teaching class, I start feeling very light, as if my feet weren't touching the ground any longer. Then I picture taking a couple of my students by their hands and bringing them with me along The Pearl String, all of us stepping over pearls, like rocks across a stream. I want to show them how much more there is beyond the First Pearl."

Clare is starting to feel very tired and uncomfortable. "You should get some sleep now," she says to Eve. Eve lies down on the couch and puts her head on Clare's lap and curls up into a tight little ball. She is shivering and her head is hot on Clare's lap. Clare shifts positions, trying to get comfortable, but cannot. She waits until Eve has fallen asleep, and then she lifts Eve's head up and places a pillow under it. Then she finally goes off to her own room to try to sleep.

Chapter Eight

At four A.M. the next morning, Clare wakes with a sharp pain in her stomach. She's had this pain on and off for a few months now, but today is the worst. She starts to get out of bed and the pain runs down her legs. She feels her forehead and knows she has a fever. She forces herself to get up and go into the bathroom. Again, for the fourth day, there is blood in her urine. She dresses quickly and places a blanket over Eve, who is still asleep on the couch. She figures she can go over to the clinic, get some medicine, and be back before Eve wakes up.

At the clinic, they immediately make Clare lie down and insist on running a series of tests on her. The nurse asks her if she wants to call someone to come and wait with her, while they run the tests. She tells them not to call anyone. She doesn't want to frighten Eve.

A few hours later, Clare wakes to the touch of the nurse taking her temperature. The nurse speaks so gently to her that she bursts into tears. She hasn't cried in front of anyone since before her mother died. The nurse wipes the sweat off Clare's head and explains that the test results will be ready shortly. Clare is worried that Eve will wake up and wonder where she is.

Actually, Eve is just now waking, back at their apartment. When she finds that Clare is not home, she assumes Clare has gone to work. She decides *she* should work as well, but she can't seem to sit down at her desk to begin.

She paces back and forth between the kitchen and her bedroom. Each time she's in the kitchen, she rearranges the food on one of the shelves in the refrigerator. On one trip into the kitchen, she alphabetizes the cookbooks.

Each time she goes into her bedroom, she swerves by her desk, on which is sitting the hefty, black notebook that contains the most recent of her many attempts at writing a dissertation. This one, like the many before it, has, just last week, been judged by her department chairman as a fascinating piece of work, but, unfortunately, not an appropriate topic for the philosophy department.

Each time Eve careens by her desk, she attempts to sit down and look at the dissertation, so she can decide where to go from here. But just as her knees begin to bend and her ass approaches the desk chair, panic overcomes her, and she suddenly straightens back up and hurries off toward the kitchen again. There she busies herself tidying the napkin drawer or putting new labels on the spices.

She hasn't been able to look at her most recent dissertation since a week ago, when it got rejected. Finally, on her ninth sweep of the bedroom, she whips the chair out from the desk and plops herself down. She shudders and takes a deep breath, hesitates, and then opens the dissertation gingerly. She reads the title page:

ON GRACE AND THE GROTESQUE

She winces and flips quickly to another page and reads a few lines from the center of the page:

Often the modes of *finite* grace are held within the form of *absolute* grace like pieces of fruit in a bowl. There are different combinations of fruit at different times. For example, at one moment the bowl may be filled entirely with peaches.

Eve feels a tightening around her rib cage as she reads, making her breathing difficult. She tries to take a deep breath, but can't, flips again to another page, but none of it makes any sense to her. She reads a line from another page:

At this level of grace, the grotesque is merely the reverse side of the coin.

Eve's whole chest feels cramped now, as if thick, wide bandages were being wrapped very tightly around her, to prevent any movement. A rush of grey wings passes in front of her eyes, and for a moment, her head falls to one side, spinning. She wipes her eyes on her sleeve to clear her vision. She keeps turning the pages rapidly, until she gets to one that contains some drawings. She sees a row of six boxes, each containing a separate diagram and numbered from left to right. The row is labeled

PENULTIMATE STAGE OF FINITE GRACE BEFORE REVELATION

But the edges of the boxes begin to look wavy and the diagrams begin to blur into one another. Eve slams the notebook shut and gets wearily up, holding the edge of desk and chair for balance, dizzy, weak-kneed.

She shuffles into the kitchen, like an old woman, sits down at the table and picks up a pencil. She wants to write a letter to her father to apologize for her heel dropping off of her shoe, but there's no paper there. Instead, she draws fat zeroes on a white paper napkin. The tip of the pencil hurts her, as it rips through the thin skin of the napkin. She takes the napkin over to the sink and runs it under the water to obscure the wan circles she has drawn on it. The napkin sinks into itself, losing its shape altogether and beginning to pull apart under the faucet. She watches its loss of shape with fascination, as it falls from its own contours and retreats into its drenched torso.

She takes the wet napkin and gently spreads it out as flat as she can on the table. How *thin* it is! She puts her ear down next to it, but she can't hear it breathing. The sweet flowers, which were once its proud border design and connoted its cheerful personality, are now no longer visible. Its features are lost. She bends down to the napkin and kisses its wet face, and then, cautiously, gently, lifts its weak body up, supporting it with both hands, raising it up to her own face and placing it over her eyes and cheeks and nose, pressing it in to fit her face exactly, like a mask. The napkin sticks there for a second and then its own weight drags it down, dribbling its water down her chin as it drops into a lump on the table.

She bends down to the napkin and sucks on an edge of it and swallows a bit of its water. But decline has taken firm hold of the napkin and cannot be reversed. It does not even know that she is lifting it up now, on a big soup spoon, and sliding it gently down into a coffee cup so it can rest in peace in its cozy grave.

Back at the clinic, Clare is given medication for a bleeding ulcer and allowed to leave, after having promised to stay in bed and rest. She has not told the doctor that she sometimes works three shifts in a row, at the busiest Italian restaurant in the Village. She decides to just take this one day off and calls in sick from a pay phone in the street. Then she goes to buy some groceries. Now that Eve is finally up again from bed, Clare wants to make her a big pot of soup.

Chapter Nine

After staring at her little napkin in its grave for quite some time, Eve resumes her pacing about the apartment, waiting for Clare to be back from work. Eve feels very tired and would like to go back to bed again, but she is afraid that if she falls asleep, she will have her spiral dream. She sees fluffy bird feathers everywhere, floating in the air like dust. They land on her lips and eyelids and get stuck there, which she finds unbearable. So she gets back in bed, in the bright daylight, her ears stuffed with toilet paper, and a black scarf tied over her eyes. She pulls the covers up over her head to keep the feathers out, curls up into a tight ball, and squeezes her eyes shut. She plans to stay awake, so that she won't have the spiral dream, and can just rest under there until Clare gets home.

At first all she sees behind her eyelids is solid black, with a few flashes of red darting across it. But when she squeezes her eyes shut even tighter, suddenly an image of her friend Kate appears in bright colors. The instant she sees Kate, Eve's stomach tenses and she starts sweating. The sweat glues the sheets to her, holding her down to the bed.

She sees an image of Kate walking very slowly up the long staircase of her house. She has seen this exact image a thousand times before. Kate is wearing a skirt and her legs are bare and freshly shaven. Kate always walked with her tension held in her calves, so her gait was stiff and rigid. She held her back very straight, as if it were in a brace, her neck barely moving. She looked deliberate when she walked, never relaxed, never just wandering.

When they were both in high school, (Kate three years older than Eve), Eve had tried to imitate everything Kate did. She had often tried to walk like Kate, but her own leg muscles were too loose and her back too slumped over.

Usually when Eve had a picture of Kate in her mind, as she often did, it was one in which Kate was walking away from her. Eve and Kate had grown up together, on the campus of the theological seminary where Eve's father was the president and Kate's father was on the faculty. Their fathers had gone to college and divinity school together and had ended up working at the same seminary. Kate, like Eve, was her father's first-born and bore a striking resemblance to him. Sometimes Eve and Kate and their fathers would stay up late into the night, discussing philosophy and theology, long after everyone else had gone to bed. These were some of the happiest memories Eve had of Kate. She and Kate used to pretend they were seminary students talking with their boyfriends in the student dining hall.

Kate was an artist and did paintings which were based on these late-night discussions. Eve would make up titles for the paintings like, "The Hideous Death of Solipsism" or, "Who Could Trust a Platonist?", titles which they both found uproariously funny.

Often when the two families were together at Kate's house, Kate would suddenly get up in the middle of dinner or a conversation and quietly go up that long staircase to her room. Eve hated it when Kate did this. She longed to run up the stairs after Kate and beg her to come back down with them. But she was always afraid of getting in Kate's way, of intruding on her. Whenever Kate suddenly got up and left like that, in the middle of a party, Eve would feel the same cramp in her stomach that she felt now.

Eve had spent many hours trying to imagine what Kate was doing up in her room alone. She pictured Kate holding one of her large art books in front of her and turning the pages, while staring past the book out the window. She could picture Kate's face perfectly at those moments because she had seen that expression on Kate sometimes when they were together. It was totally *flat*. It made her skin look pale and grey, like old dishwater. She pictured that Kate would eventually stop turning the pages of her book, let her arms fall limp at her sides, and just sit there, perfectly still, staring with a fierce concentration out the window. Her calf muscles were so tensed that her feet lifted off the bed.

Eve and Kate had spent so many evenings together, sitting and talking in Kate's kitchen. Eve ate cheese and crackers, and Kate drank coffee and smoked lots of cigarettes. Many years later, Eve could still clearly picture Kate carefully tapping the ashes of her cigarettes into very tiny containers, like bottle caps or jar lids.

Whenever Eve saw that flatness begin to take over Kate's face, she would leap up from the kitchen table and begin to do one of her routines. She would dance wildly about the kitchen, making fun of all of their friends, taking off her clothes and putting them back on upside down and backwards, gluing folds in her cheek with model airplane glue to make fake scars, or scotch-taping her eyebrows so they pointed straight up. Finally, Kate would begin laughing and the flatness in her face would go away. They would often end up getting hysterical and laughing at everything. It was at those times that Eve felt closest to Kate. She felt that she had been able to do something *useful* for Kate. They would usually end these evenings by saying certain of their favorite words, which they both found excruciatingly funny, like the word "burlap".

Eve felt relieved each time she was able to help dispel the flatness from her friend's face. But she also worried that she might not be able to do this forever. In fact, she had already seen her ability to do so becoming less and less effective. Sometimes her routines completely failed. She would get progressively more outrageous, saying sacrilegious things about their teachers and friends, but Kate would just sit there without moving, looking at Eve as if she weren't there, as if she had already left the room and was alone upstairs.

It was at those times of Kate's departures that Eve would sometimes pretend she carried Kate inside her stomach. The first time she could recall ever doing this was when she was about seven and Kate was ten. Both families were staying at Eve's family's summer cottage. Everyone was down on the beach. She and Kate were lying apart from the others, on two bright red beach towels that Kate had brought Eve as a present. Eve regarded anything Kate gave her as a precious object, and she felt very happy lying on that towel. The sun was hot and she was watching Kate through a sleepy haze.

Everyone else was down at the edge of the water about to go swimming, even their fathers, who usually stayed up in the cottage and read. Kate had said she didn't want to go swimming, so Eve had stayed with her, although it seemed so strange to her that Kate wouldn't want to be part of the excitement. Eve had been looking forward to swimming with Kate all summer.

Eve was startled when she saw Kate suddenly jump up and start walking deliberately, stiffly, down the beach. Kate turned up the path leading up the dune to the cottage. Eve felt her stomach muscles tighten. She longed to run after Kate and gently take her hand and beg her to some back and lie down next to her again on the red towels. But Eve couldn't move.

As she watched Kate climb the dune, Eve began to feel a horrible cramp in her stomach. Kate disappeared out of sight at the top of the dune. Eve could feel a hard lump in the center of her stomach. Then she realized it was *Kate* who was there inside her, and she sighed with relief. She knew she could keep Kate warm and safe in there, keep her from leaving, keep her happy. It gave her comfort to feel the weight of Kate in there, as she walked slowly down to the edge of the water and joined the others.

Sometimes Eve had also imagined crawling inside of Kate's stomach, curling up into a little ball, and riding along with Kate wherever she went. She would hug Kate from inside, rubbing her hands gently along the inside of Kate's stomach, hoping to calm her, sliding back and forth inside, as Kate walked briskly on those tight calves.

Eve worried increasingly, as the years passed and Kate went away to college, that she would be unable to sustain Kate's life in her stomach, that she would no longer be able to protect her. Sometimes when Kate was riding inside of her, Eve would feel Kate ice over and freeze in there. Then Eve's joints would ache carrying her, and a thin crust of frost would form on the inner layers of her skin from Kate's frozen breath. Then Eve would not be able to get either of them warm. This would usually happen when Kate had been taken away to a hospital. When Kate got out again, she would thaw and become warm again in Eve's stomach, warming Eve's whole body. But Kate's hospital trips were becoming more and more frequent, and she stayed longer each time, so Eve was often very cold.

Toward the end, Kate's mother would often call Eve on the phone, frantic, begging Eve to come over and perform one of her routines to make Kate laugh. Eve would race down the row of faculty houses, her heart aching, and leap into her act, snatching whatever objects were at hand and doing something ridiculous with them. She would balance egg cups on her nose, use her bra as a ribbon to tie up her hair, dance about with earrings made out of cheese dangling from her ears. Occasionally, it still worked for a few minutes, but then she would lose Kate again into that flat stare.

The last two weeks, Kate rode in Eve's stomach like a dead pebble. So Eve had crawled into Kate's stomach instead, to be nearer to her, to try to comfort her. But she had felt Kate's stomach cramp in on her so tightly, she could hardly breathe in there. Kate's tension had extended from her calves into every part of her body.

On her last day, Kate had taken a long bath, washed her hair, and put on clean, ironed clothes and fresh sheets on her bed. She had opened all the drapes and windows in her room, and then she drank some chemicals used to develop photographs. Since Eve was inside Kate's stomach at the time, she felt those chemicals come splashing down on her head, drenching her and eating wide holes in Kate. Gradually all the tension flowed out of Kate's body through the holes. For the first time in her life, Kate's calf muscles were totally relaxed. The flatness spread over her whole body. Eve looked out through one of the holes and read the note Kate had left beside the bed:

Forgive me for contaminating the wastebasket with the chemical bottles. Be very careful not to touch them.

Chapter Ten

Eve wakes from her memories of Kate and calls for Clare, to see if she's home yet, but there's no answer. She thinks of going over to the restaurant where Clare works and waiting there for her to be done. But she had promised Clare that she would work on her dissertation. Clare has been supporting Eve by working extra shifts at the restaurant, so Eve can teach just one class at the university, and spend the bulk of her time working on her dissertation.

Eve unglues herself from the sheets, takes two consecutive showers, clips her finger and toe nails, and then finally sits down again at her desk to work. She arranges her desk so that every object is either parallel, or at right angles, to every other. She has a lot of trouble deciding whether to have the sharpened points of the pencils line up evenly with each other, or the eraser ends. Neither looks quite right, so she keeps changing them back and forth until finally, giving up in despair, she settles on lining the eraser ends evenly.

She is just getting the last pencil in place when the doorbell rings. She decides not to answer it, afraid that it is one of her students, come to get her, come to see where she's been. Besides, she really wants to try the pencils the other way around, just one more time, before she begins work.

But the doorbell keeps ringing insistently, so, finally, she scoops up all the pencils and hurls them into the wastebasket, jumps up from the desk and races down the five flights of stairs to the front door. A mailman hands her a package and she signs for it and heads back up. As she makes her way up the stairs, she hears a distinct rhythm pounding in her head: three little iambs: dă D̄a, dă D̄a, dă D̄a. Then the beats become actual words, which repeat over and over, now synchronized with the rapid beating of her heart and her feet climbing the stairs. The words are

RĔ-C̄ĒP-TĂ-C̄L̄ĒS ŎF D̄ĒĀT̄H

"Receptacles of death?" she says out loud. "What the hell does that mean?"

Yet the phrase keeps pounding in her head as she reaches her apartment and sits down to open the package. "Receptacles of death," she hears, as she tears open the well-sealed package, "receptacles of death," as she is ripping off the thick twine, then the brown wrapping paper, then the tape holding the box shut, then the straw filler inside the box, "receptacles of death," then the cardboard, throwing all of these wrappings on the floor until at last she has reached what was so carefully protected. It is one wool sock.

"One wool sock?" she says out loud. "*One wool sock?* Who the hell would send me one wool sock?"

She bends down and picks up the outer wrapping, but there is no return address anywhere. She can feel her heart beating more quickly now. She doesn't want to get involved in this. But she can't help thinking about the phrase "receptacles of death" and can't stop her mind from trying to figure it all out, to make some *sense* out of the sock and the phrase.

She knows if she were smart, she would just take the damn sock, toss it into her sock drawer and go on with her work. But she can rarely leave a sock a sock. So she follows the sock to its logical conclusion. If she assumes this sock to be the aforesaid "receptacle of death", then (naturally), it follows that inside the sock will be a dead foot.

So, she reaches down into the sock with a pair of tongs and extracts a small yellow foot and drops it into a conveniently nearby salad bowl. She thinks of pouring some olive oil over the foot and dashing in some red wine vinegar, perhaps tossing some fresh dill over the top and making a nice vinaigrette. But she stops herself. She's very tempted to go further, to run down to the vegetable store on the corner and buy some Boston lettuce and an avocado and make a real salad with this foot. But she restrains herself. She has often done this in the past, and, in fact, has very much enjoyed eating that salad. But she forces herself to abandon the foot in the salad bowl and go back in to her desk.

Since she can't bear to face her dissertation, she decides to find something practical to do. She is leaving for Italy in a few weeks, so she decides to pack for her trip. She takes a suitcase down from the closet shelf and begins throwing various items into the suitcase in a frantic cascade. She looks over at the pile and notices that a leather boot is nuzzling its toe inside a pair of black silk underpants.

"Get your damn toe out of my crotch!" she snaps at the boot. She also sees a pile of pillowcases in a corner of the suitcase.

"Do I really need a dozen pillowcases in a monastery?" she asks herself. "Let's be logical. Do monks use pillows?

If so, are a *dozen* pillowcases necessary? I think not." She takes the pillowcases out and tosses them across the room.

"And don't you *dare* ask me why I'm going to live in a monastery in the hills of Umbria," she says, addressing the boot. "Ask my father, he's sure to come up with a rational explanation."

She pulls the whole top drawer out of her dresser and turns it upside down over the suitcase, thus adding to the pile lacy, pink silk slips and black nylon stockings she has never in her life worn. She runs into the kitchen and grabs both the wool sock and the yellow foot and tosses them onto the pile as well.

Chapter Eleven

When Clare finally gets home, she is very relieved to see Eve is O.K. She puts away the groceries and starts making a hearty soup and a fresh pot of coffee. She looks up at the calendar hanging on the wall and then walks into Eve's room.

"Did you remember you had a date today with Paul?" Clare asks.

"What's today?" asks Eve.

"Wednesday," says Clare. "Remember, you promised to have lunch with him today?"

Eve nods and shrugs her shoulders.

"You might as well go," urges Clare. "I'm going to take a nap. I stayed up too late last night reading. I don't have to work at the restaurant tonight, so I'm making us some soup for dinner."

"O.K.," says Eve, staring at the wool sock.

"You probably should go then," says Clare. "You're already a little late." Clare's medication is making her tired and she's anxious to have Eve leave, so she can lie down.

Eve goes into the bathroom, glances in the mirror, decides not to shower, dresses quickly, and heads over to the restaurant where she is to meet Paul. By now she is an hour late, but Paul is still there waiting for her, sipping a Bloody Mary. She has never before kept a date with him, although she has made many.

She and Paul have been fellow students in the doctoral program of the philosophy department for years and have taken many courses together. He looks quite beautiful in his perfectly-proportioned, clean, young body. Although he is two years older than she, Eve always refers to him as "The Young Philosopher" when she is discussing him with Clare. She refers to all her friends and lovers by titles, such as "Saggy Breasts", "The Hegelian", or "Green Teeth". The Young Philosopher smiles when he sees her, and by that upward curve of his lips she knows that she has him under control.

She is both excited and utterly exhausted. Her excitement has very little to do with The Young Philosopher, nevertheless it gives her a lusty charm and she can see this hitting The Young Philosopher as he stumbles off his bar stool to greet her.

At first she is very affectionate toward him, greeting him with a big hug, kissing him warmly on the neck, showing lots of interest in him and what he's been doing, making sure that he is totally devoted to her. She flips her long hair about, stares at him with meaningful expressions and gets up and saunters to the bathroom, so that he can watch the other men watching her. She orders a dry martini and raw oysters, which she slurps whole between her lips. She eats pieces of her lunch with her fingers, groaning at how good everything tastes. She congratulates herself: the pearls with her black T-shirt dress and no bra looks great. Under the starched white tablecloth her legs are clammy.

The Young Philosopher looks at her with his gorgeous, big brown eyes and his ridiculously long eyelashes and approves of her whole routine. In fact, he is feeling quite flattered.

She feels confident that she has laid sufficient groundwork now. He is all attention and they are sipping their coffee. So she begins to experiment with him a little, picking up a few innocuous ideas he cares about and twirling them a bit in the air. He keeps asking her what grade she got in the course they had taken together on The Later Heidegger. Their professor had announced solemnly in the last class that he had been very disappointed in them and that only one student had really understood Heidegger and had received an "A". The Young Philosopher is very anxious to find out if it was Eve. So she tells him it was.

"I *knew* it was you!" he says with great conviction.

"You were right," she says, smiling and shrugging her shoulders.

They had kept up a tedious argument all semester as to whether or not she had understood Heidegger. She had taken the position that she had absolutely no idea what Heidegger was talking about, and he had taken the position that she understood Heidegger perfectly. The resolution of this argument seems highly important to The Young Philosopher and seems to depend on whether or not Eve got the "A". His relief at the news is remarkable.

"So, now that you know I got the 'A'," says Eve, "you can go ahead and fall in love with me, right? Heidegger has put on his stamp of approval."

The Young Philosopher seems not to have heard this and is talking on bravely now about sections of *Being and Time*, his shyness having evaporated in light of this important news. As he is talking, she is muttering femininely supportive things like, "Yes! I never thought of it that way before. You're absolutely right!"

As he is talking, she isn't listening to a word, but keeps picturing herself taking off her string of pearls and wringing it around his hairless, white neck.

After he finishes explaining a very complicated point in his dissertation, she responds to it by saying, "Yes, good point, except for the fact that I got a 'C' in the course."

At first he doesn't seem to have heard her correctly.

"What?" he asks.

"Except for the fact that I got a 'C' in the course, not an 'A'," she says.

He looks surprised and cocks his head, puzzled.

"No you didn't," he says. "You couldn't have."

"Yes, I really did," she says. "I hate to disappoint you, but I only got a 'C'."

He thinks about this for a minute and says nothing.

"I've never gotten a 'C' before in my life," she says. "And to tell you the truth, I honestly thought I understood Heidegger."

The Young Philosopher seems genuinely upset and sorry for her. He orders two Brandy Alexanders to cheer them up. They sip them quietly. Eve smokes a cigarette in silence, looking hurt.

After a few minutes of silence, she leans over the table and whispers softly in his ear, "I got the 'A'."

He jerks his head up and looks her directly in the eyes. He starts to speak and then hesitates, not knowing what to say, staring at her, his brow furrowed, trying to discern the truth. Then, finally, he says, "You *did* get the 'A' didn't you? Why did you tell me you got a 'C'? I knew you got the 'A'."

"You were right," she says, nodding in agreement, with a very serious look in her eyes. Then she smiles, gently, and says, lifting her empty glass, "May I have another?"

He regains his confidence again and orders two more drinks. As they are drinking them, he is telling her all about his plans for the rest of the summer and the progress he is making on his dissertation. Eve starts being playful and makes fun of the waitress. She keeps waving the waitress to their table and then speaking to her with a different accent, first French, then Italian, then something resembling Russian. She can see The Young Philosopher is basking in her playful warmth, and this begins to sicken her. She makes a pun and as they are both laughing she says, "Paul, I have a confession to make. I got a 'C' in the course."

He suddenly stops laughing and stares at her, his face turning slightly red.

"This is ridiculous," he says. "Tell me what you really got."

"I got a 'C'," she says, very slowly and deliberately. "I got a 'C', Paul."

Neither of them say anything. His face gets redder. The table is uncomfortably silent. She feels ice-cold, although she is sweating a lot. Her dress is sticking to her back, but her arms are covered with goose bumps. She thinks of getting up and going home, leaving him alone at the table. But she stays. Finally she breaks the silence.

"Paul, I'm tired of this. I'm going to tell you the truth and then we can be done with this. I got an 'A' in The Later Heidegger." She pauses. "Now get the check."

He winces as if she had just slapped him. Then he shakes his head and pokes the ashtray with the tip of his cigarette.

"Do you know what I just did with the grade?" she asks him.

"Yes," he says, without conviction.

"Well, I'm very tempted to do the same thing I just did with the *grade* with *myself.* Right here in front of you. Do you think Heidegger will be able to help you discern which is the real me?"

He looks away from her, frightened now, spanning the room with his eyes, his face bright red.

"Do you really think for one minute that all I am is your *fellow student?*" she says. "That all I am is some wimp who sits here all day discussing your summer holidays and chapter three of *Being and Time?*" She pauses. "Think about it, Paul."

He looks embarrassed and says nothing, his head down, afraid to look up at her. Then his fear awakes her own, and she shudders and changes her tone abruptly and says, in a cheerful voice, "Oh come on, Paul. Don't look so morose. I'm just fooling around. Come on, let's get out of here."

She smiles encouragingly at him. She is wavering between going ahead and experimenting with him more or just forgetting the whole thing altogether. She feels very light, as if she will float up to the ceiling and crack her head if she doesn't grab on to something. So she reaches over and takes his hand. He starts to pull it away but then leaves it there in her's.

"I'm so tired," she says.

He looks so lovely right now, flushed, animated, caught unaware in the glow of health. She is tempted to go over and sit on his lap and hide her head under his cashmere sweater. It would be so safe under there.

"Let's go back to my place and talk," she suggests.

Out on the street in the bright afternoon sun, the fact that Paul is so short bothers her. He takes her hand and she lets him, but his is sticky and she is sorry she is holding it. By the time they have walked the three blocks to her apartment, she is very disappointed in him, and in herself for having invited him to come over. His innocent anticipation of being there with her, after three years of wanting to be her lover, nauseates her and revives her desire to frighten him, to experiment with other pearls.

When they get up to the apartment, Eve goes into Clare's room to see if she is home. Clare is not there, but Eve notices a blood stain on Clare's bed. She assumes that Clare has gotten her period and has probably gone out to get some Tampax or has gone to work. She takes Paul into her bedroom and sits down on her bed, motioning for him to sit on the chair beside the bed.

She looks over at The Young Philosopher and watches him as he falls slowly out of the chair and onto the floor. He doesn't even put out his hands to break his fall, so his head smacks the floor. She notices that it sounds like an egg cracked open. He begins moaning very quietly. She can barely hear him. She touches his cheek with her foot and then she is sorry and wipes off her shoe with an edge of the bedspread.

"Stop grovelling on my floor," she says to him, and these words strike her as terribly funny, so she starts laughing, repeating the words over and over. "Stop grovelling on my floor! Stop grovelling on my floor!"

"What's so funny?" he asks.

His question surprises her, and she stops laughing. She looks up and sees that he *hasn't* fallen to the floor after all, but is still sitting in the chair.

"I thought you were grovelling on my floor," she explains.

He looks confused.

"I guess we're both really tired," he offers.

She knows he is waiting for her to ask him to join her on the bed. It strikes her as rather presumptuous of him to interject how he's feeling and to assume he knows anything about how she's feeling. What does his opinion have to do with anything?

"Look at my upper lip," she says, as she makes her lip begin twitching. Gradually she makes the twitches shift location, appearing in different parts of her face. He watches her closely and then says, "Stop it, that looks horrible."

"I can't help it," she says, controlling the twitches with perfect precision.

"Something is about to happen," she says. "Something very, very different. We're right on the edge of it. Can't you feel it?"

"No, not really," he says. He is frowning. He starts to say something, hesitates, and then goes ahead and says, "Maybe you should take one of your tranquilizers."

"Tranquilizers?" she asks. "*Tranquilizers?*" She starts laughing again.

"What makes you think I want to be tranquil? What possible effect could a tranquilizer have on this? Do you really think for one minute that a concrete, little item like a tranquilizer could stop what is about to happen? You obviously have no idea what's going on, which is just as I should have expected."

She begins singing very loudly, an unmelodious tune, without words, just "LA LA LA LA LA LA LA LA LA LA" louder and louder, until the room fills with it and all the objects in the room are suspended in her song, as if in a thick liquid.

"I better leave so you can get some sleep," he says.

"Oh, perfect!" she says. Then she sings a trill, "LAAAAAAAAAAAAAAAAA! You want me to get some sleep? How thoughtful of you, Paul. You're so concerned, so finite, so trite. Get out of here will you?"

"Listen," he says quietly and very sweetly. "I don't understand what you're going through, but I think you should get some rest."

She laughs a short laugh, like a cough, and then it lengthens out into a musical note, and as she is singing, she is wondering how long he will sit there waiting for her to stop. She continues singing for quite some time, weaving other noises into her song, like groans and barks. He looks away from her, stares down at the floor, and waits for her to stop.

The song has become a long, curving tunnel for Eve, and she wants to see what's at the end of it. So she keeps following it out, running it through, leaning into the curves so that she can round them faster, and then she sees a light at the end of the tunnel, and just as she is about to reach it, she trips and loses her breath. She stops singing and looks up at The Young Philosopher and is very surprised to see that he is crying.

"What are you doing here?" she asks him. Then suddenly she becomes tender to him.

"Go home now," she says. "I've been up for four days, I'm just very tired," she lies to him, offering him a reasonable explanation to hold on to. "I'll be O.K. I just need to sleep. Go on. I'll call you tomorrow."

"I'm worried about you," he says.

"Don't worry," she says, trying to lighten the tone of the conversation. "I'm fine. This happens to me all the time. Don't take it so seriously!"

She gets up from the bed and hands him his books. He moves very slowly toward the door. If he doesn't get out of here in a few seconds it will be too late. She has never in her life seen anyone move more slowly. Her patience is rice-paper thin. She wants to kick him out the door and throw his copy of *Being and Time* out after him. But she forces herself to be patient and to wait. When he is finally at the door, he turns around and looks at her. She twitches her lip just faintly.

"I'll talk to you tomorrow," she says, with a quick smile.

She closes the door and locks it, is sure she sees a bit of his finger caught in the door, but she leaves it there and races back to her bed and hides under the covers.

Chapter Twelve

Eve waits for a long time under the covers, until she is sure Paul is gone, and then she jumps out of bed, fills a bucket with two cups of Mr. Clean and hot water, grabs a scrub brush and runs to the door. She looks for Paul's finger, but it's no longer there, so she scrubs the door where she had seen it. Then she runs back into her bedroom, yanks the bed out from against the wall, and starts vigorously mopping the floor under the bed. She pulls off the sheets, pillowcases, and mattress cover and takes them into the bathroom and throws them in the tub with four cups of Tide and scalding hot water. She takes a broom and stirs the hot, soapy water, swirling it in large circles until the tub is full. Then she goes back into the bedroom and takes the mattress off the bedframe and vacuums it and washes the wooden bed. Then she washes the chair in which Paul was sitting earlier, going over every inch of the chair three times and then drying it with towels. She finds a red beach towel with the other towels and holds it up close to her cheek, feels a deep sorrow well up in her, and a cramp in her stomach.

Everywhere she looks she sees little white dots. She fingers the pearls around her neck and washes the dots away as best she can, scrubbing everything in the room, over and over again. She keeps coming across her father's tie and tries to clean off the dots on it so that there will be no more pins sticking into him under those dots. But the dots remain—they are sewn into the tie, part of its design, its texture, its plan. But she doesn't give up—tries every cleanser in the house on those dots.

After Eve has given up her cleaning for now and has finished putting clean sheets on the bed, she notices a row of her students curled up next to each other on her bed, like five letter Cs, five new moons stacked and waiting for use once a month, waiting for the right day and tide. They are her five, favorite students from the Intro to Philosophy class she taught this past semester, five young women, who banded together forming a circle around her wherever she went, following her everywhere, like young animals in a pack. They used to sit for hours with her in her office, listening to her talk about her current dissertation, about the later Heidegger, about the songs of birds, about her lovers. Often she took them home with her, and Clare would cook dinner for all of them and they would stay up till early in the morning talking, then falling asleep, one by one, on the couch and floor. When they were all asleep, Eve would rise and carefully cover each one, place a pillow under each of their heads, and then go into her room to sleep alone.

Then one day, after the course ended and summer began, Eve suddenly abandoned them. They couldn't find her anywhere, left messages in her office and at home, called her day and night for weeks, but she wouldn't answer them. Clare became annoyed at having to take their increasingly frantic messages. Eve found a room in the basement of the administration building at the university. It was filled with old furniture, broken desks and cracked blackboards. She hid there, in the far corner, behind a barricade of blackboards, arriving early in the morning, so no one would see her, and leaving late at night. There she worked on her dissertation alone.

At first she found herself worrying that her students would find her and she would have to look into their eyes and respond to their questions.

"Why did you leave us?"

"Where have you been?"

"How could you be so mean to us?"

But she forced herself to keep working, and gradually she thought of them, and everyone else, less and less. Her thesis, *On Grace and the*

Grotesque, had grown longer and longer. It was already over five hundred pages. She had lost track of its original purpose and theme but kept writing, and drawing endless diagrams and charts.

She had begun spending the night in her little room in the basement, working until early morning, sleeping a few hours and working again. She wouldn't tell anyone where she worked, especially Clare, knowing that Clare would come there and take her home and make her eat and sleep. Her face had become grey, her energy drained, and she found it increasingly difficult to leave the room, to make it up the stairs and home on the subway.

Now she reaches her arms out to encircle the women on the bed, to crawl in with them and hug them, to comfort them and tell them she will never leave them again. But they are gone, and her arms fall through empty space, hit the bed limp, encircling nothing.

The phone rings and it is Clare. She tells Eve that she is fine, but that she is going to have to spend the night in the hospital. She tells Eve that visiting hours are over, and not to worry, that she will be home the next day. Eve hangs up the phone, still thinking of the five new moons, and then panics when she realizes that she has forgotten to ask Clare what was wrong, why she was in the hospital. She grabs the phone to call her back and then realizes she doesn't know what hospital Clare is in. She puts the phone back down, panicking, crying, furious at herself. She remembers the blood stain on Clare's bed, runs into Clare's room and removes the stained sheets and replaces them with the clean sheets from her own bed.

Chapter Thirteen

Within a few days, Clare's medication has begun to take away some of her pain and the bleeding has stopped, so she has gone back to work. Eve has been doing her best to take care of Clare, but it makes Clare even more uncomfortable. The same day Clare goes back to work, Eve finds herself feeding a huge spoonful of something cold and grey into the mouth of a skinny, paralyzed geriatric in the city mental hospital.

Later, Eve carefully washes the patients' wrinkled, stale bodies, patting them dry with clean towels, dressing and feeding them. Later she rushes home, after two hours at the hospital, disgusted at the smell she carries on her. At home she washes herself for a long time in the shower, then scours out the shower, changes the sheets again on the bed because she thought she saw a dark hair on one, and then falls exhausted into her bed.

The first week at the hospital, Eve works two hours a day, but she remains unsatisfied. By the end of the third week, she is up to eight hours a day, including weekends.

The woman in the volunteer office, through which Eve works, keeps asking her if she is sure she can spare all this time. Eve assures her it's O.K.

One night when Eve stumbles wearily in the door, Clare is there waiting to talk to her. "You don't need to do this, Eve. You're fine. You don't have to go this far. You need to work on your dissertation this summer so you can teach again full time."

"I know," says Eve. "I just need to do this for a little while longer. Please. Then I can work on my dissertation again."

Eve starts a project at the hospital, making one of the basements into a recreation room for the kids in the adolescent ward. She cleans the basement out alone at night. Two of the nurses from the adolescent ward offer to help her on their days off, but Eve says she's almost done. She tells them not to come down yet, that she wants to surprise them. She is afraid they will see how much more work there is to be done, and then she'll have to think of an explanation for why she wants to do it alone.

She talks the night guard into letting her stay there in the basement very late to work. She wants to finish this project before she leaves for Italy. The guard begins hanging around while she works, glad for the company. He offers to help her, and, finally, she lets him. Together they fill huge cartons with old bits of broken furniture and piles of moldy newspapers.

Joseph is fifty-five years old and has a limp in his left leg. Eve would much prefer to do the work alone—she can't stand seeing him limping across the floor dragging the heavy cartons. But she knows he really wants to help her, so she lets him. She helps him drag the cartons up the steps and out to the trash area.

Eve saves some of the old furniture to use and cleans it up with some rags and cleanser, which Joseph slips to her in secret. He is pleased with the progress they're making and talks on and on about his life as they work.

One night Joseph excitedly brings Eve an old rug and a large folding table he has discovered in the basement of another building at the hospital. They shake the heavy rug outside, and Eve beats it with a broom while Joseph holds it up. Then they drag it back inside and Eve sweeps it, over and over.

"It's a beauty!" she says, smiling at Joseph. He is very proud of his contribution.

When the basement has finally been cleared out and swept, Eve and Joseph take turns mopping the enormous concrete floor. It takes them hours, since they have only a small sponge mop to use. When they are finally done, they each take one end of the rug and lay it in the center of the floor and place the rescued furniture on it. They grin at each other, pleased with their work, and give each other a hug.

The next day Eve brings her record player and all of her records to the basement room. She buys bright posters for the walls and makes curtains for the small, high, basement windows.

She decides to christen the room with a party. She buys Cokes and huge bags of Fritoes and potato chips. She arranges a time with the nurses, and everyone on the adolescent ward, who is not bedridden, comes. Eve puts on some records and dances with the patients and fixes them up with partners.

Most of them are highly medicated and move very slowly, but they love the music. Eve dances with an eighteen- year- old boy who wears a football helmet because he repeatedly bangs his head against the wall. His neck is very skinny and weak and the helmet is too heavy, so his head lobs back and forth as they dance.

Chapter Fourteen

A few days after finishing the project in the basement, Eve brings one of the girls from the adolescent ward in the hospital home with her for the day. Clare is cooking in the kitchen when Eve arrives with Charlene. Clare looks worried when they come in. Eve is trying to be especially cheerful because she really wants Charlene to have a good day. Charlene hasn't left the hospital for over two years because there was no one to take her out. Even on the holidays, when almost all the patients were checked out on passes, Charlene stayed there on the ward and watched T.V. with the nurses.

Charlene is seventeen and weights 285 pounds. She has two children, whose pictures she immediately takes out of her large, black patent leather purse and shows to Clare. Clare mumbles approval and busies herself with the soup she is making them for lunch.

Charlene wants to be a hairdresser. She has been practicing for years on the nurses and anyone else who will let her. She asks Eve if she can do her hair.

"Sure!" says Eve. "That would be fun."

"I'll need a few things," says Charlene. She tells Eve what she needs and Eve goes down to the drugstore, leaving Charlene in the kitchen with Clare. Charlene begins telling Clare her life history, in no logical order: how she had to push her husband off the fire escape because she saw him about to throw a brown paper bag down into the trash in the alley below and she knew her baby was in there. She keeps talking non-stop until Eve returns half an hour later.

Eve places the supplies on the kitchen table: a bag of large, pink plastic hair rollers, hair spray, bobby pins and a hair net. Charlene sets to work on Eve's hair, talking on about the time she shoved her father down the basement stairs of their house, when she was seven, and he broke his neck.

When Charlene has finished setting Eve's hair and sprayed it stiff with the hair spray, she goes over to the soup, smells it and dips the spoon in to try a taste. Clare looks up from the cookie batter she is stirring and takes the spoon from Charlene.

"It's not done yet," says Clare. "I'll give you some when it's done."

Charlene turns on the radio very loud, still talking about events from her life, and begins dancing.

"Charlene's a great dancer," Eve says to Clare.

"So I see," says Clare, as she turns the radio down a little.

Charlene *is* a good dancer, always in perfect time with the music, her large body flexible and her movements fluid.

"How can she hear the music when she's talking so loud?" Clare shouts in Eve's ear. Eve shrugs her shoulders. Her head is itchy. She tries to scratch under the rollers. Her hair is wet and sticky. The room smells like hair spray and cream of carrot soup.

"When do these come out?" Eve yells to Charlene, trying to be heard over the music. But Charlene has her eyes closed and is singing loudly along with the music and doesn't hear Eve's question.

"I love this song!" she yells. Eve waits until the song ends and then she turns down the radio and asks again.

"Can we take these out soon? My head itches."

Charlene feels the rollers.

"I think they're ready," she says, professionally, and begins hurriedly pulling the rollers out, pulling out pieces of Eve's hair in her rush. She brushes Eve's hair into a tall, sticky mound.

"I'm going to give you a 'Beehive'," she says.

"Great!" says Eve.

Eve's hair stays wherever Charlene puts it, glued there by the hair spray. Charlene places the hair net over the mound. She pulls out a strand from each side and makes a little curl around her finger.

"Do you have any tape?' she asks, turning to Clare.

"I don't think so," says Clare.

"I have some on my desk," says Eve. Charlene is holding the curl around her finger and is looking impatiently at Clare. Clare reluctantly puts down the soup spoon and gets the tape. Charlene puts four or five pieces of tape over each curl.

"Can I look now?" asks Eve.

"Not yet," says Charlene. "Wait till I take the tape off."

"You're going to love it," says Clare.

Clare sets the table for lunch and serves Eve and Charlene each a bowl of soup.

"Aren't you having any?" asks Eve.

"No, I'll have some later," says Clare, who is still feeling a bit nauseated from her medication.

Charlene bends her head down so her nose is almost in her soup, sniffing it suspiciously. She takes a small spoonful.

"Is there herbs in here?" she asks Clare.

Clare nods.

"I can't eat no herbs," says Charlene. "They make me throw up."

Eve stirs her soup spoon in circles in her bowl, while Charlene keeps talking and eats most of the cookies Clare has just taken out of the oven.

After lunch, Charlene removes the tape from Eve's curls and proudly watches as Eve looks in the mirror.

"It's fabulous!" says Eve. "You've got a great career ahead of you!"

Eve longs to take off the hair net and wash her hair before taking Charlene back to the hospital on the subway, so no one will see her like this. But she doesn't want to hurt Charlene's feelings, so she leaves it as it is. She puts the rest of the cookies in a bag for Charlene to take back to the hospital. Charlene eats them all on the subway.

"Can't take these into the ward," she says to Eve, her mouth bulging. "Them patients is vultures over cookies."

Chapter Fifteen

When Eve gets back from taking Charlene to the hospital, she is exhausted. Clare is not home, and Eve lies down right in the middle of the kitchen floor. The linoleum feels cool and smooth, like a cheek, against her cheek. She lies there for a few minutes, rubbing her own cheek gently back and forth on the floor, with her eyes closed. She can feel something beginning to change within her. She begins to grow calm and doesn't recognize this feeling—it's as if she were a different person, as if she were inside someone else's body. After a while, she becomes convinced that she *is* in the body of someone else. There's something very familiar about this body, but she can't quite place who's it is.

She lies on the floor for a long time, letting this change take place fully within her. Then she opens her eyes and slowly raises her head up off the floor. As she begins to stand up, she finally recognizes who she is—she is the Virgin Mary. This realization floods her with a surge of joy, although it is in no way surprising to her. It is just a simple, wonderful, physical fact: *she has Mary's body.*

This pleases her tremendously, and she gets up from the floor very, very slowly, wanting to take note of every single one of Mary's movements. If only Clare were home now to watch Mary with her and help her remember all of the details!

Eve moves delicately, afraid that if she moves too quickly, she will shake Mary off, like a feather stuck to her by friction.

She slowly raises both her hands and gently touches Mary's forehead, her eyelids, her nose, her cheeks, her lips, her chin. She smells Mary's fingers, puts the tip of her tongue on Mary's fingers, one at a time, and then licks her palms and examines her skinny wrists and the back of her hands with their veins protruding. Then she walks carefully toward the hall, feeling the weight of Mary's arms and the folds of her skirt rubbing against her legs as she walks.

Eve goes into the bathroom and stands in front of the floor-length mirror. She gasps in horror when she sees Mary's hair in a tall, sticky mound, under a black hairnet. She removes the hairnet and runs Mary's hair under the water from the faucet in the bathtub, scrubbing out all the hairspray and taking great care not to get Mary's clothes wet. Then she towel-dries Mary's hair and combs it back flat against her head and ties it in a tight rubber band. Then she goes back in front of the mirror and begins to undress Mary, watching her every movement in the mirror. Each gesture is incredibly slow and careful.

First she takes the ring off Mary's finger. Then she carefully removes Mary's sandals, her bracelet, and the string of pearls around her neck. Then she watches as Mary pushes each button through its buttonhole, until at last her blouse slides open and Eve can see Mary's breasts.

They are the most beautiful, perfectly-shaped breasts Eve has ever seen in her life. Mary's skin looks young, soft and smooth, and she has a faint bathing-suit line around her breasts. Eve reaches out to touch Mary's breasts, and is startled when her hands hit the cold hard mirror.

Eve takes off Mary's skirt and watches it fall into lovely folds around Mary's ankles. Mary steps out of the skirt and turns to hang it neatly over the edge of the sink.

Then Eve catches her breath as she watches Mary take off her underpants. Mary slips the fingers of both hands under the top of her white lace panties and lowers them very very slowly. Eve can barely breathe as she watches in the mirror. She looks Mary directly in the eyes as Mary continues to lower her panties. Mary holds the waistband open in an oval while she steps gracefully out of the panties.

Then Eve watches as Mary begins to turn around and around

slowly in the mirror. First one way, and then the other, continuously moving, round and round in circles, in a slow deliberate dance, the circles getting smaller and smaller.

As Mary circles, Eve can see that Mary's back is large and wide. She touches it with her hands, staring back over her shoulder into the mirror to watch. Mary's legs are long and thin and lead up to a small round ass. Her legs are smoothly shaven and must have been recently rubbed with lotion because there is a shine to them.

Mary stops turning. "I'm getting dizzy," she says to Eve.

"I will put you to bed," says Eve. She walks slowly into her bedroom and smooths the sheets, fluffs up the pillows and tucks Mary in.

PART TWO

Assisi, Italy

Chapter One

"Surely Saint Francis didn't eat this well, did he?" wonders Eve, as she watches one of the monks drenching the tomatoes on her plate with a thick, golden olive oil and another placing a juicy chunk of roasted veal on her plate, adjacent to a mound of pasta. Her question is answered by comparing the monks' tripled chins and bulging robes to the skinny elbow of Saint Francis, which is poking into her leg under the table. She purposely drops her fork and leans down to have a look under the table. Saint Francis is there, in his brown Franciscan robe, picking up crumbs that have fallen to the floor.

"It's *you!*" she whispers, grabbing hold of his hand and squeezing it tightly, her heart leaping for joy. Francis is weary from having begged for thirty-six hours straight, with little success, so he can barely sit up. Eve motions for him to lean back against her legs to rest. The long, white folds of the tablecloth hide him from view. Every few minutes, Eve reaches her hand down under the tablecloth and strokes Francis' head gently and hands him some bread.

After dinner the monks invite Eve to join them in their evening prayers in the chapel, but she declines, saying she will go to her room to rest and do a little writing. They nod understandingly, having had many writers come to stay in their guest hotel to rest. The monks' cheeks are bright red, and as Eve looks from one face to the next around the long table, she cannot tell them apart. Their fat has drowned their individual features, and they do, in fact, all look like brothers.

After the monks and the other guests have left, Eve sneaks back in and looks under the table, but Francis is gone. She goes up to her room in the guest hotel, takes off the brown robe (which the monks offer to all of the guests to wear while they are there), and puts on a short black skirt and a bright pink top. Then she rushes up the street to a cafe to meet Claudio. Claudio lives in town with his mother and works in the guest hotel helping the monks. He has offered to show Eve around the city.

When she sees Claudio at the cafe, he looks even younger than he did this morning, when she first met him. She had thought he was about fifteen, but now he looks closer to twelve. She watches his little ass as they walk along the street and figures she could probably cup the whole thing in one hand. He looks like he could be her son, one of the few blond Italians in Assisi, blue eyes the same shade as her's, slim-hipped and tall for his age.

As they walk about the town, Claudio showing her the sights, they stop at various cafes and Claudio buys her little glasses of Sambucca with dark coffee beans floating in it. She wonders if he is old enough to drink, but she encourages him to join her and watches as his face grows more flushed with each drink. She can't really tell if he is drunk, since he continues to move so agilely through the winding streets and alleys, leading her up the mountain, toward the castle that sits above the town.

They sit down in the tall grass and wildflowers on the side of the castle, just outside the city wall, looking out over the plains. Eve stretches out on the grass, and Claudio lies down next to her, barely coming up to her shoulder. She leans over and kisses him on the lips and is pleased to find they are smooth and soft, like a woman's. At first Claudio is surprised by the kiss, but soon he is kissing her anxiously all over. His tongue is small and delicate and his breath is sweet, like a young child's.

Claudio nuzzles his head between Eve's breasts and his cheeks are very smooth, not a single whisker has yet appeared. He sucks gently on Eve's breasts and she wishes she had milk in them for him.

86
●

She unzips his pants and strokes him, as they roll a little down the hill and then catch themselves, laughing. She finds she can hold his whole penis in her mouth quite easily. Claudio is licking and nibbling her everywhere. He reminds Eve of a little goat.

As they roll slowly down the hill, they leave a trail of clothes and crushed flowers behind them. Eve thinks she sees a bony arm reach out to touch her from behind a bush, but she closes her eyes and rolls quickly past it. She sees a yellow wildflower caught in Claudio's hair, and she presses her face up close to it, breathing in its fragrance to steady her.

Back in New York, the first night Eve was gone, Clare had dreamt that Eve's plane had crashed and large blood-colored waves had engulfed her. Clare woke up screaming and cried on and off the rest of the night. She had never cried like that in her life. In the morning, she felt strangely calm. The second night, Clare was again wakened by a dream, but she was not frightened. In this dream, she had seen Eve rolling down a hill in the embrace of a young boy. The dream made her angry at Eve, and she had spent the rest of the day recollecting things Eve had done in the past that only now, in Eve's absence, made her angry. She was surprised that she had not been angry at Eve when these events had originally occurred.

For the next week, Clare's anger grew into a rage at Eve. At night her dreams were filled with horrible things happening to Eve, like Eve's lips being sewn together with a fishing hook and wire, or one of Eve's patients at the hospital pushing her off the top of a twelve-story building and Eve falling into a pile of broken glass in an alley below.

After about a week or so, the rage toward Eve died down and Clare had another dream, which she would often remember in the years to come. In it, she saw Eve spinning wildly around in circles, downward, through white, whirling clouds. At first, Clare was frightened, but as she continued to watch Eve spinning, she felt a peacefulness seeping into both her own body and Eve's. From then on, Clare slept more soundly, and during the days, she felt increasingly well. The pain in her stomach began slowly to fade and a new energy began to rise within her.

Chapter Two

Early each morning, Eve dresses in her brown Franciscan robe and joins the monks who have already been praying since before dawn in their little chapel. Today, she trips on the edge of her robe as she enters the chapel, and bumps her head on a pew. The monks look up briefly, and then bow their heads again. She stumbles into one of the pews and kneels down. Her robe begins itching terribly, and the more she tries to ignore the itches, the worse they get. So she slips her arms out of the sleeves and scratches herself under her robe as inconspicuously as possible.

Eve follows along with whatever the monks do, now reading from the Bible, now singing, now praying again. She finds that while they are singing, she can scratch more vigorously without them noticing.

She looks about the chapel and notices that someone seems to be missing. She can't place who it is. She counts the same twelve round heads that are always there in the dining room. But she keeps looking around as if she were supposed to meet someone here but had forgotten, for the moment, who it was.

The monks are reading from their Bibles again. Eve can't really follow what's being said in Italian, since the only Italian she knows is a few lines from Dante's *Inferno*. The monks are reading so quietly, she is afraid she will disturb them by involuntarily blurting out some kind of loud noise. She keeps taking deep breaths, scratching herself and trying to relax.

Suddenly she coughs, just once, and a fat glob of phlegm lands on the open Bible in her lap. She looks around to see if anyone has noticed, but luckily their eyes are closed in prayer. She lifts the Bible up very carefully, so that none of it runs off onto the pew or floor, and tiptoes out of the chapel. Once out, she races down the hall to the bathroom and turns the Bible upside down over the sink, shakes the phlegm off and then carefully wipes that page with a damp paper towel. But the page is stained, and the stain has actually seeped through to a few pages below, where the spot is paler yet still visible.

Eve begins to panic, not knowing how to remove the stain, not knowing what to do. If Clare were here, she'd know what to do. Should she try to put soap on it? But she figures that the pages are too thin and would tear. She thinks of just closing the Bible and returning it to the chapel, but she knows that someone will open it, see the stains, and know that she is the one who left them there.

She stands in the bathroom, the Bible shaking in her hands, sick to her stomach, afraid someone will come in and catch her with the stained Bible open in front of her. She thinks of throwing it in the wastebasket, but then someone will find it and see those pages and report her to the monks. So she decides to take it up to her room and hide it there. She peeks out into the hall, and seeing no one, races to her room, where she wraps the Bible in a towel and hides it under her mattress and then runs back down to breakfast.

The monks have already started eating, and she sits down without looking at up anyone. She is afraid a piece of food will jump out of her mouth and land on one of the monk's round cheeks. She tries to eat more slowly, but can't seem to slow down. The monks take this increase in appetite as a good sign and keep refilling her plate with more bread and cheese.

After breakfast, the monks go off to their jobs in the guest hotel, the gardens, and the kitchen, and Eve rushes back up to her room. She removes the Bible from under her mattress, and her heart sinks when she finds that four of the pages have been glued together by her sticky phlegm. She slams it shut and wraps it in a paper bag and takes it out into the street with her. She drops it behind a bush when no one is looking and hurries off to a little grocery, where she buys four huge chocolate bars and a box of plain, white cookies.

She scurries back to her room, tears open the cookie box, unwraps the chocolate and places a hunk of chocolate between two of the cookies. She devours all of the cookies and chocolate, in this same sandwich formation, within a couple of minutes. She feels sick to her stomach, disgusted at herself, and then, within moments, ravenously hungry again.

In a tiny cafe, in little Italy, Clare holds her spoon suspended in the air as she is absorbed in looking at David, whom she has just met a few days ago.

"You haven't eaten a bite," he says, smiling.

She smiles and knows, in the very center of her heart, that he is the most wonderful man she has ever met.

"Let's go," he says, taking the spoon gently from her hand. He pays the check and they walk leisurely back to his apartment. He makes a pot of tea and they sip it quietly, and then Clare puts her head on his lap and falls asleep. David falls asleep too, his hands cupping Clare's head.

Chapter Three

Eve has stayed inside all day, afraid the monks know about her phlegm in the Bible and embarrassed to see them. Finally, she gathers up her courage, dons her brown robe again and tucks her long hair up under the hood. She tiptoes out of her little room and heads for the Basilica di San Francesco, her eyes lowered and her hands folded in front of her. She wanders about the enormous church, trying to be incognito, stopping to kneel for a few seconds in front of different altars, glancing at the frescoes that line every wall, looking about longingly for something she can't quite seem to locate.

Eventually she winds her way up to the upper basilica and then gasps when she sees a long series of frescoes depicting the life of Saint Francis. As she moves slowly along the wall, carefully studying each scene from his life, she gets warmer and warmer, until sweat begins dripping from her forehead. She removes her hood and shakes out her long hair, but keeps her hands folded, so sweat drips from between her clenched fingers. When she reaches the far end of the room, she sees a fresco of Saint Francis preaching to the birds. As soon as he begins talking to them, their chirping dies down. Their wings flutter for a moment longer and then fall still too. Eve sits down in a pew in front of the fresco and listens to Francis' sermon. One of the birds lights on her knee and remains there, perfectly still, both of them absorbed in the sermon.

Francis is talking about how lucky the birds are to be able to sing and fly through the blue skies day after day. He sits down on a tree stump, and the birds surround him, getting as close to him as they can, so as not to miss a single word. Eve moves closer, too. Francis is talking so softly now she can barely hear him. She lifts the little wooden pew and moves it right up next to the wall and stands up on it to get closer. The sweetness of his voice makes her dizzy, and she almost loses her balance and falls off the pew. His words take her breath away. She reaches up to the fresco and touches his robe.

"Where were you?" she asks him. "I've been looking for you everywhere!"

He looks down at her tenderly and continues talking to the birds. She stands up on her toes and puts her head on his lap. He strokes her hair as he continues talking to the birds. He is talking about Brother Sun, how generous he is, how grateful the birds should be for the gift of his warmth. Eve can feel Brother Sun beating down on them, but Francis' robe remains cool against her cheek. She reaches up and takes his hand and holds it tightly, hoping he won't take it away. He finishes his sermon, gently removes his hand from her's, gets up, and walks slowly off, all the birds following him.

Suddenly a monk comes rushing toward Eve, yelling in Italian, shaking his finger at her and pointing to the pew and the fresco. Eve jumps down off the pew and runs out of the basilica, leaving the monk trailing far behind. She tries to avoid the stares of the shopkeepers as she runs through the narrow, winding streets back to her room.

By the time she gets back to her room, she is drenched in sweat, her face sheet-white, gasping for breath. There is a knock on her door and she jumps up, startled. She opens the door and sees one of the monks looking at her with a worried expression. He asks her if she is all right, but she finds she can't speak to him because there is already another sound coming from her mouth. Eve tries to assure him that everything is O.K. and that he shouldn't worry, but the sounds are beginning to take what's left of her breath away. Short yelps, like a little dog trying to bark, are coming from her mouth.

The monk gets Eve a glass of water and some of the other monks come in to see what is happening. Eve takes a gulp of the water and it flies out of her mouth, like spit, onto their robes.

Eve is very ashamed at disturbing the monks' silence with this spectacle, and finally the yelps die down and she catches her breath and lies down on her bed, silent at last.

The monks are standing around her bed in a circle, staring down at her. She doesn't know what to say to any of them, so she jumps back up out of bed, thanks them and apologizes (in English, which none of them understand), trying to explain that she is fine and that she will go out and get some fresh air and take a walk.

Chapter Four

Eve hurries out into the bright afternoon sunlight, still wearing her robe, and when she is safely out of sight of the monastery, she lifts her robe up around her knees and breaks into a run. She looks frantically in all of the cafes for Claudio, but he is nowhere to be seen. She figures he must still be working in the hotel, but she is afraid to go there to find him because she might see one of the monks. She longs for Claudio's sweet, boy tongue; she's grown accustomed to meeting him when he is through with work. She feels safe with him. Each day, he has shown her different mountain paths, leading to open fields of yellow and white wildflowers and beautiful ruins of castles. After a while, they always lie down on the bare ground and make love.

She stops in a little clothing shop in the first piazza and buys a very tiny French bikini and a bright red beach towel, which she wraps around her waist, over the bikini. She rolls her robe up carefully and puts it in the shopping bag and heads toward the public pool. The stones of the street are hot and burn her bare feet, making her realize that in her haste to get away from the monks, she had forgotten to put on her sandals.

When she gets to the pool, there are a dozen men, sitting around the edge of the circular pool, sunbathing and drinking. There are no other women there, and Eve makes her way quickly to a little patch of grass on the far side of a hedge. She spreads her new towel out and lies down quickly so that she is hidden from view behind the hedge. A straight-pin holding the price tag on her towel sticks into her foot. The sun burns her white skin, but she is afraid to move. She is very thirsty, but doesn't dare walk past the men to the bar in her tiny bikini and has nothing else to wear but her monk's robe.

Before long, one of the men, whom she has heard the others calling Mario, comes over to her and offers to buy her a drink. She refuses, but he insists. They spend the rest of the day, and on into the night, drinking, and, later, dancing on the little dance floor next to the pool. Eve dances with with her eyes closed, her head thrown back, twirling round and round. She begins kissing Mario as she dances and later pulls him over behind the low hedge, where they make love on the red towel, only a few feet away from the dance floor.

Mario falls asleep after they make love, and Eve gets up quietly, so as not to wake him, and dances with other men, sticking her tongue into each of their mouths as they dance. She feels them rise against her and she desires all of them, chooses one named Giorgio, and leads him off into a nearby field. Later, she takes other men to the same spot in the field, where the grass is matted down, fits her ass into the same indentation in the ground, still damp from the man before.

In the morning, still wearing her bikini, Eve brings Mario to the hotel to get coffee in the coffee shop where Claudio works. When Claudio comes to take their order, he is very happy to see Eve and smiles at her, but she pretends she doesn't know him and orders him around rudely. She snuggles up to Mario and puts her tongue in his ear while Claudio is serving them their coffee. Claudio looks like he is about to cry, and she gets up and takes him over to the corner and whispers in his ear,

"Go suck on your own mother's breasts. I'm sick of you. Don't ever speak to me again."

She turns to go back to Mario. Claudio grabs her hand and tells her he has a present for her. She notices that he looks about ten.

"Here," he says, and reaches into his pocket and hands her a small white box. She opens the box and takes out a tiny gold locket, in the shape of a heart, on a gold chain. She takes the locket and walks back to the table where Mario is sitting and drops the locket in her cup of coffee.

Claudio follows her and picks up her cup and feels around in the coffee with his fingers until he finds the locket. He stands there, holding the locket dripping with coffee, speechless, staring at Eve. Eve's cup rattles in his hand.

"You're spilling my coffee," she says to him. "You better be more careful."

Then she turns away from him and hurries out of the hotel. Mario pays the check and runs out after her.

Chapter Five

When Mario gets out in front of the hotel, Eve is nowhere in sight. He looks everywhere for her, goes back inside and looks in the coffee shop again, but she has vanished. He finally gives up and drives off angrily. After he has left, Eve sneaks out of the little chapel where she has been hiding and runs upstairs to the second floor of the hotel, where Adriana, the maid, is cleaning the rooms. At Eve's request, the monks have given her the job of helping Adriana clean in the mornings.

Adriana looks up from the floor she is mopping, frowns and shakes her finger at Eve, points to Eve's bikini and shakes her head and motions her away to change her clothes. Eve starts to leave and then remembers she has her monk's robe in her shopping bag and takes that out and puts it on over her bikini. Then she bends down on her hands and knees beside Adriana and helps her mop.

They dip small white squares of cotton, the size of handkerchiefs, into a pail of clean water and wash the floor bit by bit, refilling the pail with clean water every few minutes. Eve is impatient with this method of cleaning and would like to take the whole bucket and pour it onto the floor and slosh the water around with her arms and legs and feet. But Adriana has been cleaning these floors for forty years the same way and has no interest in other possible methods.

When they finish the floor, Eve hurries to the little cupboard between the beds so that she can reach the chamberpot before

Adriana. She knows Adriana hates to empty the chamberpots, so she always tries to get to the cupboard before her. Often Adriana rushes up behind her and says, "No, no!" and takes the chamberpot from Eve and does it herself. But this morning she lets Eve do it.

Eve carefully carries the full chamberpot down the hall to the bathroom. This one must have been used twice during the night. When she reaches the bathroom, she pours the warm, smelly urine into the toilet, spilling some on her hands. Eve feels faint. She goes to the window and opens it. But there is no air today. It is hot, still, and humid. She looks down into the street and sees Saint Francis leaning against the building, watching her, so she hurries back to her cleaning.

Today, to Eve's surprise, Adriana lets her do *all* the chamberpots. With each one, Eve gets more worried. Does Adriana have a relative who works at the pool? Does she smell men under Eve's robe? Did Claudio show her the locket dripping with coffee?

By the end of the morning, the smell of the different urines has seeped through Eve's robe and into her skin. When they have finally finished cleaning the last room, Eve races back to her own room and takes a long cold bath (there is no hot water here), but the smell remains. After her bath, she puts her bikini in the metal wastebasket and sets fire to it.

In New York, Clare and David are lying on the couch, browsing through last Sunday's *New York Times*. Clare has not heard from Eve since Eve left for Italy, although she has written Eve a number of letters. She used to check the mail anxiously each day for news from Eve. But now she is staying at David's most of the time, and just goes back to her apartment to check the mail once or twice a week. Last night Clare dreamt she saw Eve change into a white bird whose wings caught fire and then flaming spun down to the ground.

Chapter Six

For many weeks now, Eve has wet the grasses, prayed in chapels, scrubbed floors with white cotton squares, and sung hymns in a language she does not understand. One night, stars brilliant overhead, she suddenly lifts her head from the grass to look over the shoulder of the man on top of her. She peers through a tunnel that suddenly opens in the grasses and sees Saint Francis standing perfectly still in front of a dark cave. She raises herself up on one elbow, the man on top of her pounding her hip bones into the ground beneath her, and watches Francis. He seems to be waiting for something. He is staring up at the sky.

Eve looks up too, sees only the black night bright with stars, looks back at Francis and sees him now staring fixedly at both his hands, and then falling down on his knees. Eve starts crying, wants to rush up the hill through the opening in the grass and comfort him, take him in her arms, look at the holes in his hands. The man on top of her lets out a loud groan and rolls off of her. She jumps up and runs through the grass, but can't find the opening, loses her direction, runs down the hill a ways, then up again, looking for Francis, but finds only grass blowing in the cold, night mountain air.

She hears the man coming toward her through the grass and runs over to a clump of bushes, slides on her belly down under the bushes and waits there until the man passes, passes again, passes again, and then heads off down the mountain, yelling her name and swearing.

When his footsteps can no longer be heard, Eve peeks out from under the bush, sees no one and slides back out. She is naked in the cold air, searches about for her clothes in the dark, but can find only her bra and her skirt, no blouse. She looks again frantically for the cave where Francis was standing, but can't find it. She wants to stay there for the night, but knows she must get back to her room while it is still dark, before someone sees her with only her skirt and bra on.

All the way down the mountain, Eve hears crying. It gets louder as she follows the winding path down the hill. Beside an abandoned peasant's hut, she sees an old woman lying on a stone in front of the door. The woman is shivering with cold. Eve has nothing to cover her with, thinks of taking off her skirt to wrap around the woman, but she has nothing else on under her skirt. She hurries over to the woman and motions to her to wait there, that she will be right back.

Then she runs down the hill as fast as she can, her arms crossed over her chest, trying to cover herself should she meet anyone along the way, running so fast in the dark that she trips and falls three times and cuts open one knee. The blood runs down her leg. When she gets back to her room, she wipes the blood off, dresses quickly, takes all the blankets and sheets from her bed, fills her suitcase with clothes and grabs her purse. On the way back up the hill, she stops at a store just opening for the day and buys a huge bag of food. Then she runs back up the path.

She is disappointed when she gets back to the hut and sees that the woman is not there on the stone in front. She opens the door to the hut and finds the woman curled like a worm on a bare mattress on the floor, in the corner. Eve goes over and touches the woman's forehead. It is very hot. She makes the bed with her own sheets, the way she learned working in the hospital, making one side first, and then carefully sliding the woman over on the sheet and making the other side.

She takes out a bottle of water and pours a little on a clean handkerchief and puts it to the woman's mouth. The woman stirs and opens her eyes. She smiles at Eve as if she had known her all her life and expected her to be there. Eve holds the wet cloth up to the woman's lips and then gently pats her face with it. A fine grey dust comes off on the cloth. The woman shudders. Eve puts her blankets over the woman and tucks her in.

She tears open a loaf of white bread and takes a tiny piece from the soft center of the loaf and puts it to the woman's mouth. The woman opens her mouth and Eve sees that she has no teeth. She takes the bread and dips it into the water to soften it and then places it in the woman's mouth.The woman swallows it and closes her eyes. Eve continues to feed her little bits of the bread and water, on and off, all day long.

At night it gets colder, and the woman's fever rises and she shakes all over. Eve has no more blankets to cover her with, so she takes off her own clothes and gets in bed with the woman and holds her against her. The woman's body has shrunken to the size of a seven-year-old's, her skin shrivelled and loose on her bones. Eve stays awake all night listening for the woman's irregular breathing.

At dawn, just as the sun rises, Eve falls asleep for a few minutes. When she awakes, the woman is cold and stiff in her arms.

Chapter Seven

Eve follows behind one of the monks as he carries the old woman, like a baby in his arms, down the hill. Eve is weeping, can't seem to stop, her head pounding in the heat of the sun, words pounding in her head and through her limbs, beyond her mind, as they wind their way down the narrow mountain path toward town. The words ring loudly, like a bell clanging in her head, her own inner keening, her head become heavy with the sound, too heavy for her thin neck, so it falls to one side.

"Rivulets, trees, grass in patches," she hears in her head, "slopes, streams, caves, birds calling, falling, stigma, stigmata, a blemish, a taint, a spot, a scar, a hole, red speck, the sun, the hole, the blood, nerves open, a red speck falling, a song, a warning, a bell tolling, rising, falling, a fever, a prayer, a prayer, a prayer..."

Later that night, earth covering the mouth of the old woman, the words gone from Eve's head, Eve sits at dinner with the monks. She notices that the skin above her lip is twitching, but this time she can't seem to control it. Then her cheek starts twitching, too. She wipes her cheek with her napkin, trying to smooth out her skin so the monks won't see it twitching. Then her shoulders start shaking, and she gets up from the table and runs out into the garden. She falls into a row of cabbages, her whole body in a spasm, cramping her into a round ball, like another big, fat cabbage.

She tries to get up, but she can't uncurl her limbs; they are clenched shut, her whole body a tight fist. One of the brothers comes out to find her, sees her in the cabbages and calls another brother, and they carry her into the little chapel, still curled up, and lay her down on one of the pews. They cover her with a blanket and suggest she pray there quietly until she feels better. Then they leave her there alone. She doesn't want to be left alone, thinks maybe she is dying, calls in a whisper for Clare.

Later, Eve wakes up back in her own room at the hotel, having dreamt that the monks had come into her room while she slept, humming the *Dies Irae*, kissing her legs and arms, their vile breath suffocating her. She recalls having prepared the sacraments for them in her dream. She had taken the thin wafers and flavored them by sticking them inside different openings in her body. The wine she had made from the blood of a dead cat she had found in the garden, under the wide zucchini leaves.

She looks up and sees one of the monks reading his Bible at her bedside. He looks over at her and smiles, then reads to her from the Bible in Italian. His voice is too sweet and makes her nauseated. She pretends to fall asleep again and waits until he finally leaves her room. Then she gets up. Her body is covered with garden dirt, stinking of compost and fertilizer. She goes over to the basin of water to wash herself. She blames the monks for this dirt, imagines they have kept her from washing for the two months since she arrived, figures it is part of her initiation rites, to make her grow foul like them. She cups her hands to her mouth and blows into them. Her breath smells like their's. She sees a dead fly and three black hairs in the basin and cannot bring herself to use that water. She sits back down on the bed, takes the Bible the monk has left open for her on her table, and scribbles invectives in it. Even the Bible smells; it is limp and grey, the color of the old woman's skin.

Chapter Eight

Ever since Eve first arrived in Assisi, she has been coming across short pieces of white string wherever she goes. One day when she noticed her hand was clenched tightly around something, she opened it and was startled to find a three-inch piece of the cotton string, curled like a worm in her palm.

She saves these pieces, brings them back to her room, and meticulously records in her notebook the time and place she found them.

She has seen them more and more frequently each week. Sometimes when she lifts her head from the pillow in the morning, a piece rides along, hooked to one of her ears. Once, in the evening, when she went to brush her teeth, there was one draped lyrically over the handle of her toothbrush.

She lines each one of these strings up in a row on her bedside table. They are different lengths, but none longer than six inches. She makes a note of the shape they were in when she found them, whether curled, straight or bent. Then she carefully straightens out each piece and lines them up, parallel, on the table.

One night, after she has just taken off her blouse in a dark passageway behind the Basilica di Santa Chiara, one of her lovers suddenly bursts out laughing and asks her why she is wearing a string around her neck. She reaches up and is surprised to find another piece of the string tied around her neck, a weightless necklace.

She has begun to feel that the bits of string mark out a trail ahead of her. She follows the strings like clues, like arrows, going in whatever direction they point. She sees a piece encircling her glass of Sambucca, pointing in the direction of the chapel. In the chapel, she sees one on the kneeling cushion, pointing to her room. As she enters her room, another falls off the doorknob and catches on her wrist.

Sometimes, when coming upon one, she hears herself whispering affectionately, "Little Pearl String!" This always surprises her because there are no pearls on these strings. They have apparently slid off the ends of the string and fallen down between the bricks in the street, where she cannot see them.

Often Eve makes entries in her notebooks in which she attempts to analyze these strings. Tonight she writes:

I am now positive that these pieces of white string have been taken, bit by bit, from one long, endless ball of string, which resides elsewhere. The pieces appear to me at perfectly chosen moments, to guide me, to keep me in line. Finally I have come to believe that there is always more string, that these small, finite pieces maintain their *Absolute Form* elsewhere, and merely allow themselves to appear to me in these truncated bits, curled beneath rugs or caught on the branches of trees, as reminders that there is always more.

As Eve is writing, a dozen unopened letters from Clare slide out of her notebook and fall down behind her bed. In her concentration, she hasn't noticed the letters falling. They remain in the dust under her bed, until, weeks later, Adriana finds them when she is cleaning Eve's room, after her departure, and one of the monks mails them to her in New York.

On her last day in Assisi, Eve goes for a long walk through the town. She wears a short red skirt, showing her long legs, bronzed at the pool, and her hair, which is now bleached the color of sunlight and which has grown down below her waist, flies out in a wild torrent behind her.

As she passes the cafes and bars, the men sitting outside drinking call to her as she passes, "Bella! Bella!" She hurries by them, turning into streets she has never taken before. All the streets begin to look the same, and she loses her direction, winds and circles, round and round. She can't find her way back to the monastery. She passes the same cafe three times, the men calling to her more insistently each time she passes, "Bella! Bella!" One man gets up and follows her, asking her if she would like a drink. She hurries away from him and breaks into a run. He follows her and she runs faster. She ducks into an alleyway and hides under a staircase, where there is a white hen tied to a post by a thin white string.

After the man passes by, Eve comes out again and keeps walking, looking for her way back to the monastery, but she can't find any familiar landmarks. She is afraid to speak to anyone, afraid to appear lost, so she keeps walking stiffly through the streets, her legs freshly shaven, her calf muscles tensed.

The streets circle round one another, her head is spinning, bella, bella, she's running now through the streets, passing the same corners, again and again, bella, bella, spiralling, spinning, fainting, bella, bella...bella, bella.

PART THREE

New York City

Chapter One

During the plane trip back to New York, Eve keeps taking more and more clothing out of the suitcase under her seat and putting it on: a long skirt over her mini-skirt, knee socks and boots, a long-sleeved shirt, a turtle-neck, a huge scarf and a large baggy sweater. Just before getting off the plane, she puts on her raincoat and a wide straw hat. She carries her suitcase in front of her like a shield.

When she gets off the plane, Clare runs up to her, pushes back her hat, laughing, saying, "Are you under there?" and kisses her on the cheek and hugs her tightly.

"You don't need all of those clothes on here, Eve. It's *ninety-three* today," she says, smiling as she helps Eve remove her raincoat. Eve lets Clare help her take off some of her clothing, and Clare puts it back in Eve's suitcase.

Eve has rehearsed a speech about how her trip has been a deeply-moving religious experience, with quotes from the *Psalms* and the *Canticle of the Sun* to substantiate her claims of a transformed life. She tells Clare how she has vowed celibacy, and she spells out the rigorous daily observances she has planned. She plans to rise at 4 A.M. and pray in silence in a little chapel she plans to make in her bedroom closet.

Clare listens quietly and holds Eve's hand as Eve talks frantically about her newfound peace, waving a lighted cigarette in her other hand.

That afternoon after Clare goes to work, Eve can't sit still and goes over to the philosophy department to see who's around. The only person there is Ethan, one of the adjunct professors who teaches with her.

"You're back!" he says when he sees her and gives her a big hug. He takes her hands and dramatically examines both palms. "No stigmata?" he asks, feigning shock.

They go off together for a few beers in a local bar. Eve hasn't talked to anyone in English for months, and all the words sound wrong to her, so she keeps anxiously checking Ethan's face to make sure she is making sense. She is rambling on about the infinite possibilities in all things, The Pearl String, spirals, birds and Saint Francis. Ethan keeps teasing her, telling her that she has a "disease of the mind": this passion for thinking philosophically, for wanting to explore her "infinite possibilities". After his third beer, he is yelling loudly at her. People in the nearby tables are listening to them.

"There are no possibilities!" he yells. "I've been studying philosophy for twenty years and I know. You're deluded, you're really sick, Eve, I mean it. I used to be like that, too, but I cured myself. Everything is exactly as it appears on the surface. No more. No less."

"I can prove you're wrong," says Eve. "Take that guy up on the T.V.," she says, pointing to the T.V. above the bar.

"Yeah, so what?"

"Well, for one thing, he's wearing a fake nose. Not the whole thing, just a little piece of Silly Putty along the upper ridge, just enough to change his appearance from night to night, just enough so that most people won't even notice the difference. But it's plain to me. I noticed it right after I read Bradley's *Appearance and Reality* in that "Philosophy of Mind" class we took. He changes it a little bit each night. I'm positive about this because when I first noticed it, I called him at the station and told him I knew what he was doing, and he said I was the first person who had noticed and that he had been paid a lot of money by some perceptual cognition program at Harvard to wear this putty on his nose."

Ethan starts laughing. "Fuck you," he says. "Let's talk seriously."

"Seriously?" says Eve. "*Seriously?* I've never been more serious in my life!" She says this with such vehemence that she believes it herself for an instant, and after that it doesn't matter any more. She keeps telling Ethan more details about this perceptual experiment, quoting various current philosophers of psychology, while Ethan is getting more and more angry, yelling at her louder. Finally he gets up and calls a friend and asks him to turn on his T.V. and see if the newscaster is wearing Silly Putty on the edge of his nose. After talking with his friend for a few minutes, he slams the phone down and returns to the table.

"What did he say?" asks Eve.

"He said he couldn't tell."

Eve smiles and nods her head knowingly, as if that had proved her point beyond the shadow of a doubt. Then she arranges her face so that she now takes on the look of someone Ethan has gravely insulted by accusing her of not telling the truth. By the time they leave the bar, Eve has switched into her Virgin Mary guise, striking beatific poses, her complexion shimmering and other-worldly, as if the Archangel himself had licked her clean of this world's vulgar disbelief.

Despite his anger at Eve, Ethan has been taken in by her disguises and finds himself apologizing to her as they leave the bar, although later he can't remember what he was apologizing for.

"You were right," he says. "I'm sorry. See you later." He waves good-bye and hurries off toward his office.

Eve returns to her apartment as if she were a nun returning to her cell in the convent, having just performed some ghastly chore with grace and humility. She begins to believe this, so she treats herself as if she were a nun. She hides her genitals from sight as she undresses and wears a bathing suit while taking her shower. She carefully averts her eyes as she washes and dries herself and dresses in a white nightgown she hasn't worn since her mother gave it to her when she was in eighth grade. Just before getting in bed, she puts her hair into neat little braids.

The next morning, after breakfast, Eve writes in her journal:

I woke this morning strangling in an old nightgown, like a strait jacket, which I tore off and tossed into the trash. By a happy coincidence, the nightgown landed in such a way that

117
•

it draped over the wastebasket quite musically, curving around a grapefruit half, so I had to forgive it for attempting to strangle me.

Later, when I stood in front of the full-length mirror to floss my teeth, I was surprised to see that someone had put my hair into hideous little braids. " Who the hell has been here?" I asked myself. I figured probably it was the halitosed nursemaid who chatters sometimes with the cleaning woman, gossiping about me, saying I am a "criminal", a "philosopher", a "tart", a "snob". I don't know who to believe.

All I ask of life is total lucency and consonance of thought. But every time I sense the possibilities for growth, the branches break, and the innocent growth I had begun is interrupted by trenchant theorizing. Words are the caustic slices which undo my branches, bring blood and white plant ooze.

I see now that I have no other recourse now than to traipse back from the end of each sentence to its beginning, searching for where it originated in my mouth. I do this by keeping my eyes on the period at the end of the sentence and then running backward toward the mouth, as quickly as possible, searching for the origin of its meaning...

Eve wants to read some of her writing to Clare, but Clare is always at David's. Actually, Eve is glad to have more time alone now. She wants to get to work on a new dissertation she has in mind. It is titled *The Infinite Possibilities in All Things* and has as its central metaphor The Pearl String. Eve is so excited about working that she decides to disconnect the phone. She checks the kitchen and sees that there are plenty of canned goods, so she won't have to leave the apartment for quite some time. She is glad that Clare is living over at David's now. She finds their conversation very distracting when she's trying to work.

It's nice to have the whole apartment to herself. Now she can lay her large notebooks all over the floor, opened to specific charts and diagrams. In one corner of the living room, she lays out the strings she has brought back with her from Assisi. She hopes the birds won't take any for their nests.

Chapter Two

Weeks ago, as penance for deceiving him in the bar, Eve had offered to give a lecture in a seminar Ethan is teaching. Tonight she is supposed to lecture on the ontological proof for the existence of God, a topic she had become so immersed in she had almost drowned while she was a student once in a divinity school. For some reason, she dreads giving the lecture, despite the fact that she knows the material better than she knows her own address.

Eve is shuffling through stacks of papers and notes on the ontological proof. She is having trouble looking directly at the notes. She puts on her dark glasses, but she is still unable to focus on them. The notes frighten her. She knows somehow they are connected with something she has been preparing for for a long time, something she is getting closer and closer to. She wants to call Ethan and tell him she is sick and can't do the lecture. Despite her fear, she is drawn forward.

She puts the notes in her briefcase and takes a long hot bath, washes her hair, and slowly shaves her legs and under her arms. But she can't concentrate, and she cuts herself twice on each leg. She can't really understand why she is so nervous. Obviously, it isn't the fact that she has to lecture. She's done this same lecture many times—she could give it in her sleep. No, she feels like she is poised on the roof of a twelve-story building, inching her toes closer and closer to the edge. Her head is spinning, and, just for a split second, she finds herself inside her spiral, heading down toward the bottom.

She cuts her leg again and the spiral disappears. Her legs are bleeding. She puts Band-Aids on all her cuts and gets dressed. Nothing fits right. Everything itches or is too tight. Finally she gives up on finding something comfortable and hurries off to the seminar.

During the first part of the seminar, Ethan lectures on the moral proof for the existence of God. Eve tries to focus on what he's saying, but she's jittery and feverish. She hopes she is merely coming down with the flu and that nothing more important is about to happen. But she knows it's not true.

As she is trying to listen to Ethan, trying to plan what she will say, the words

EVERYTHING...OR...NOTHING

keep repeating in her head, over and over. She understands these words perfectly, not just as words, or even as ideas, but as clear choices for what she will do tonight. She knows she must make a decision, that she must chose between doing *Everything* or doing *Nothing*. It is as clear and concrete a choice to her as the choice between doing the laundry or doing the dishes.

She desperately wants to do Everything, but she is afraid. At first she thinks that her fear is that she is inadequately prepared to do Everything. Then she realizes, with a sudden swell of panic, that, on the contrary, her fear is that she *is* adequately prepared and will thus have to face Everything.

The whole time Ethan is lecturing, Eve is shifting back and forth between choosing to do Everything and choosing to do Nothing. She can barely stay seated in her chair. Ethan's students keep looking over at her.

When Ethan finishes his part of the seminar, they break for coffee. Eve leaps up from her chair and asks Ethan if she can speak with him out in the hall.

"You look awful," he tells her.

"I know," says Eve. "Listen, something strange is happening to me tonight. I can't explain it to you now, but all I know is that I have to do either Everything or Nothing tonight, and since I don't feel prepared to do Everything, I have to opt for Nothing. I couldn't possibly do anything in between."

Ethan looks worried. He feels Eve's forehead.

"I think you're coming down with the flu. You have a fever. You better go home and go to bed." Eve is quite pale and is swaying back and forth. Ethan puts his arm around her and leads her down the hall.

"Come sit down in my office," he says.

"It's as if you had planned a twelve-course French dinner," explains Eve, "and you hadn't bought all the proper ingredients. So you couldn't make what you had planned. So you decide to cancel the dinner party all together, rather than going ahead and doing something in between, like serving a tuna casserole."

"Oh God! No tuna casserole in my seminar," says Ethan. "I won't allow it. You need to go home and rest. I'll do something else in the seminar. Is Clare home?"

"Maybe," says Eve. "I think I was supposed to meet her there tonight after class."

"Let me give her a buzz," offers Ethan. As he is calling Clare, Eve paces back and forth in his office.

"She's home waiting with a bottle of aspirin," reports Ethan. "You shouldn't take this philosophy shit so seriously, Eve. It's bad for your health. They should put a warning on the front of every philosophy text for people like you. Will you go straight home now?"

"Yes," says Eve. Ethan hugs her and watches as she breaks into a run halfway down the hall.

Eve runs as fast as she can all the way to the subway. She is afraid something will start happening before she gets home to Clare. Things are already starting to change slightly on the subway. She notices that the man sitting across from her has plastic lips. She wonders why more people aren't noticing his lips.

"Is it possible that I am the only one on this train who knows his lips are plastic?" She looks around and is astonished to see that, in fact, she *is* the only one.

"He's fooled everyone else!" she thinks. She looks at his wife, sitting next to him. By the way the woman is calmly reading her newspaper, Eve can tell she doesn't know about her husband's lips.

"Can't she tell? Even when she's up close? What about when they're kissing?" Eve wonders. "I am probably the only other person in the world who knows this fact," she concludes. She wants to tell the man that she knows the truth about his lips, but she is at her stop now. She runs up the steps of the subway, three at a time, and races all four blocks to her apartment where Clare is waiting for her.

Chapter Three

Eve bursts in the door of the apartment and runs up to Clare. "Do I look different?" she asks.

"No," says Clare. "Just tired and pale."

"That's all?" asks Eve, in disbelief. "But what about these...these fruit, or whatever they are?" She is pushing something away from her, swatting at the air as if there were swarms of insects around her.

"What fruit?" asks Clare.

"These!" says Eve as she tries to clear the air around her with both arms. "They're all around me, bulging in my air, fat fruit and vegetables, you know, like before, huge eggplants and pumpkins, remember? They've been here before."

Clare nods.

"Out of my way, pumpkins!" Eve shrieks. She finds the word "pumpkin" hilarious and starts laughing. Then she says the word "burlap" five or six times, laughing and coughing at the same time, almost choking. "Get out of here!" she yells at the vegetables, as she spins around the room, waving her arms wildly. "I have important work to do here tonight. You're in my way."

Clare grabs one of Eve's arms to stop her twirling. "Ethan said you were coming down with the flu."

"The flu?" asks Eve, surprised. "You mean...*influenza*?" she laughs. "In-flu-en-za?!" she repeats, through peals of laughter. "I thought Ethan understood that something was about to happen

...Everything...or...Nothing. I guess he didn't get it. I should have known. What do you think, O Sensible One?"

"I think I'll make a pot of coffee," says Clare, releasing Eve's arm. Eve has stopped laughing, her face gone very solemn.

"Clare, will you help me tonight? Something very important's about to happen. It's already begun. I'm scared. Will you help me?"

"What do you want me to do?"

"Just stay here in the First Pearl and hold a lantern so I can find my way back. OK?"

Clare sighs again, hesitates, and finally agrees. When she returns to the living room with the coffee a few minutes later, Eve is sitting on the couch perfectly still, staring at something across the room.

"What are you staring at?" asks Clare.

"There's something moving over there in that row of trees," says Eve, pointing across the room at the bookcase.

"What is it?"

"I can't tell."

"Well, what's it look like?" asks Clare. Eve looks around the room, describing what she sees.

"Well, I'm standing in the middle of an open field of short, dry, yellowish grass. Across the field is a row of large, tall trees. It is very hot here," she says as she begins removing her clothing. "Very, very hot, even though the sun has just set and it's growing dark. I'm sure something's moving in those trees." She is pointing and squinting her eyes to see better. "What do you think it is, Clare?"

"I don't know," says Clare. "I can't see it."

"Oh, look! It's coming out into the field now," says Eve. "It's some kind of large, hairy animal. It's walking this way. It's heading straight toward me." She pauses, and then bursts out, "It's a wildebeest! I'm sure it is."

"What's a wildebeest?" asks Clare, taking down the dictionary from the bookcase and looking it up. She reads the definition, finding it hard to picture.

"What's it look like?" she asks.

"It looks horrible. It has big horns...it's...it's running straight toward me! It smells awful. There's dust rising all around him. Help me, Clare! He's going to run me over!"

"Do its horns curve downward and outward?" asks Clare, still reading.

"Clare, it's trying to kill me!" Eve drops to the floor and covers her head with her arms. She stays down on the floor for a few minutes until she is pretty sure it has passed, and then she cautiously gets up, looking all around her. She has taken off all her clothes now and her whole body is covered with sweat.

"I almost got killed by that animal. Is he gone?" she asks, still looking anxiously around the room. "I could feel his damp, stinking breath on my back, he ran so close to me. He was so big!"

Clare closes the dictionary and gets a cool, wet washcloth and a faded red beach towel from the bathroom. She places the washcloth over Eve's forehead, and wipes some of the sweat off Eve with the towel and then wraps it around her shoulders. "What's happening now?"

"The wildebeest is gone. I can go forward. Into the woods behind that row of trees."

"Are you sure you want to?"

"I have to see what's in there."

"Why? There might be more animals. Why don't you turn around and come back here?"

"I can't turn around. I have to find out what's in there. Oh, look! There's a little path going into the woods. That must be where the wildebeest came from."

"I don't think you should go in there," warns Clare, shaking her head. Eve keeps heading straight for the woods.

"Where are you now?" asks Clare.

"I'm walking along the path in the woods."

"What's it look like?"

"The trees are getting closer together, the path narrower." Eve turns around and looks back over her shoulder. "I can't see the open field any more. The trees have closed in behind me. It's getting darker as I walk. It's very damp and humid in here." Eve is looking all around her, straining to see in the dim light. There is thick grey-green moss all over the ground and growing up the sides of the trees. Everything is obscured in a dark grey light. She kneels down on the floor and begins jabbing at the carpet with a pencil.

"What are you doing?"

"I'm digging up this moss. I need nice big pieces so I can drape them over my shoulders. I need to feel them against my skin. Ah. There." She presses the moss hard so it will stick to her skin. "It's so nice and thick, like a layer of fur, a pelt!"

Clare stares at Eve's naked body, trying to picture it covered by moss.

"I can barely see now," says Eve, looking up at the ceiling. "There's no opening to see the sky. The trees are woven together now at the top. Is it night?"

"Yes, it's night."

"Look! There's some kind of black hole up ahead. It's a cave!"

"Eve, you don't need to go into that cave tonight," says Clare. "Let's go to bed; I'm really tired." She takes Eve's hand and tries leading her toward her bedroom. Eve snatches her hand away.

"I have to go into that cave," she says firmly. "Here, hold this moss." She begins removing the pieces of moss from her body and handing them to Clare. Clare reaches her hands out to take the moss, but then she feels awkward waiting to take something from Eve's empty hands, so she folds her hands in her lap.

"I'm entering the mouth of the cave," says Eve. She reaches her hands out to touch the wall of the cave. She finds it damp and warm. She walks slowly into the cave, her hands holding on to the ridges in the wall to steady herself. The floor of the cave is wet and slippery, so she has trouble keeping her footing. She rounds a bend in the cave and, looking back, finds that the entrance to the cave is gone from sight. It is almost pitch black now in the cave. There is a very familiar smell in here, but she can't quite place it. It smells like her breath, her urine, her hair. It smells like *her*. The wall she is holding onto continues to curve, as she makes her way deeper into the cave. She can tell that she is going downhill now because she slips and slides down a ways. The walls are getting much wetter. There is a slippery fluid coating them. Eve scrapes some off in her hands, smells it and tastes it.

"What are you doing?" asks Clare. Her voice startles Eve.

"I'm in some kind of dark underground tunnel," Eve says, finding that she is beginning to have trouble speaking. Her mouth is dry and the words feel strange on her tongue.

"A tunnel?" asks Clare, anxious to keep up a conversation with Eve, to keep in touch with her.

"A tunnel...curving down into the earth. I'm going down more quickly now. It's getting steeper, more slippery. Oh, what's this?" Eve reaches down to the ground and picks up the heel of a sandal, but it slips out of her hand. She bends down and tries to find it, but it has slid down farther into the tunnel. Instead she finds a long piece of white string running along the floor of the tunnel, but can't find the ends in either direction. She follows the string with her hands and it leads her deeper down.

"What did you find?" asks Clare. No answer.

"Eve, what did you find?"

"My white string," she says, the words "white string" sounding very odd to her. "I'm following it. It's leading me down." She is holding onto the string, following it, hand over hand, as it winds its way down the tunnel.

"It sounds like you're going down inside your spiral," says Clare.

"My spiral?" asks Eve, as if she's trying to remember what those words mean.

"Yes, your spiral. In your dreams, your drawings, your fingernails, you know."

Eve is nodding her head up and down, muttering. It is almost completely dark, so she has to rely on her touch and smell to tell her what's there. She lets go of the string for a moment and reaches out to pick something up from the floor.

"What is it?" asks Clare. "What are you holding?"

Pause.

"What did you pick up, Eve? What is it?"

"A bird."

"A bird? What kind of bird?"

"A dead bird. A little dead bird." She hugs it against her breast. "A little dead sparrow."

"Is it a sparrow?" asks Clare, not knowing what else to say.

"It couldn't breathe in here. There's no air to breathe." Tears are falling down her cheeks.

"It's O.K." says Clare, gently. "It's just a bird. Birds don't live very long."

"I didn't want this bird to die," moans Eve. She holds the sparrow up close to her cheek. Her tears wet its feathers. "It was such a sweet little bird...a very young bird." She continues crying softly, rocking the bird back and forth. "I didn't want this bird to die." Clare puts her arm around Eve.

"Don't worry," she says, whispering in Eve's ear. "It's O.K., Eve. It's O.K."

"It's not O.K. at all," says Eve. She rocks the bird for a long, long time, humming to it. "Oh Clare," she says, her words coming slowly and with great effort. "I thought I knew what sadness was...when I was back there in the First Pearl...but I had no idea...like when Kate died I was so sad...but from here I see that...that I had no idea what sadness was. How...*thin* and...*diluted* my sadness was back there. It can hardly be called by the same name as this." She holds the bird's beak up to her breast to feed it. Clare says nothing, her head bent down, listening to Eve singing to the bird.

A few minutes later, Clare is surprised to hear the tone of Eve's voice change completely. It grows bright and Eve exclaims, "How sweet this bird is! How beautiful and perfect!" Her face is suddenly very different, glowing now, radiant, joyous. "I love this bird!" She jumps up and begins dancing about the room, singing a lively, cheerful song about Brother Sun, holding the bird high over her head. Suddenly she stops, arms still above her head.

"How joyous I feel, Clare! 'Joy' doesn't even seem the right word, because I used that word when I was back where you are to describe something so...so watered down compared to this...so incomplete. Look at this amazing little bird!" She holds her empty hands out for Clare to see. "Oh Clare, if you only knew how different this is...what I'm experiencing now...things are getting purer and more complete as I move down this tunnel. Why was I so afraid of going down my Spiral before?" She looks down at the string on the floor of the tunnel. "Oh look! There are pearls on my string! It's my Pearl String! My Pearl String is leading me down my Spiral! The two sisters have joined

128
●

together!"

Eve can't stand up any more and has to crawl on her hands and knees. It's getting increasingly hotter as she makes her way underground. She tries to respond to Clare's questions, but no words are coming to her. The most extraordinary expressions are coming over Eve's face, unlike any Clare has ever seen: at one moment the look of ecstasy and bliss, and then, seconds later, excruciating pain. Farther down her Spiral, comes the look of hope, switching suddenly to a look of horrible despair.

At one point, Eve suddenly screams and grabs something from the floor in front of her. "Daddy's tie!" she yells, shaking the tie frantically in the air and then placing it across her heart, between her breasts, holding it tight against her chest. Those are the last words she utters for a long time.

It is quite cold in the room and very late at night, yet Clare can see Eve's whole body is still glistening with sweat. Eve is rounding the turns of her spiral more quickly now, for the circles are getting smaller here near the bottom. The tunnel is so narrow now, that Eve can no longer crawl on her knees, but must slide along on her belly, pulling herself down.

Just as she is about to reach the bottom tip of the spiral, to reach the very last pearl on the string, she stops and hesitates for a second. A current of terror enters her feet and runs through her entire body and out the top of her head. Then with a final thrust of energy she stretches her arms out in front of her as far as they will go and touches bottom.

A gasp unlike any Clare has ever heard bursts from Eve's mouth. Eve's body freezes for a moment, every muscle tensed, her arms stretched out in front of her, her legs rigid out behind her, toes pointed, as if she were in the middle of a perfect dive, suspended in mid-air above the water. Then, a split second later, it is over and her body goes totally limp.

"What happened?" asks Clare. Eve is lying absolutely still on the floor of the living room. Clare jumps up and bends down to see if Eve is breathing and to take her pulse.

"Eve, what happened just then?" asks Clare. Eve does not respond.

"Eve, are you all right?" Clare is yelling now. Eve finally lifts her head up off the rug, blinks her eyes, and looks up at Clare. In a faint, barely audible whisper she says,

"I did it!" Then a long silence. "I made it...to the end of the Pearl String!...the bottom of my Spiral!...I was there!" She is grinning now as she slowly gets up off the floor and makes her way over to the couch. She closes her eyes again and leans back against the couch pillows, still grinning.

"What was it like?" asks Clare.

But Eve cannot speak for quite some time. When she does finally speak she speaks very slowly, as if trying to remember the right words in a foreign language.

"Everything...was...there," she says, whispering. "Everything... everything at once...every pearl...every possibility...everything... everything in its complete form...with nothing missing."

"What do you mean?" asks Clare. "What was it like?"

"It was like...like...*wholeness*...like knowing wholeness...being whole...knowing the whole ball of string...the whole Pearl String...the whole Spiral...all at once." She pauses, trying to remember exactly. "Everything was there. Nothing was missing." She closes her eyes remembering, trying to savor it. "Everything...and...Nothing, they were both there...I knew them both...they're the same!...and I thought they were different before. It was so wonderful, Clare, because I wasn't *suspecting* any more. I *knew*. I was there. I lived there."

"What did it look like?" asks Clare."What was at the very end of the Pearl String?"

"A flash...a bright flash of white light...of all colors at once!...and then it was gone. It was so short. I didn't want it to end. I wanted to stay there. It was the best place in the universe. It's where I've always wanted to be. How good it felt. Like I was finally *home*! But it was so short." She opens her eyes and looks around the room. A puzzled look comes over her, as if she doesn't recognize anything in the room. Her eyes move as she looks slowly around the room and then at Clare.

"Were you here the whole time?" she asks. Clare nods. "Holding the lantern for me?"

"Yep."

Eve pulls the towel over her bare knees. She sits quietly on the couch, thinking about what has just happened. Then, suddenly, she exclaims, "Oh my God! Clare! I think I'm already heading back to the First Pearl! Is it true? It can't be. Is it, Clare?"

Clare nods her head. Eve leaps up and starts pacing frantically back and forth in the room. "No!" she insists. "I won't go back. I can't stand to live back there again. I want to stay where everything was whole." She begins to panic and starts crying and screaming. "Oh, shit, I'm already beginning to forget what it was like out there at the end. It's already beginning to fade. But it was so bright. So clear." She is starting to talk faster and faster. "I'm coming back so fast. It's not fair!"

"But you have to come back," says Clare quietly. "You can't live there. You could only be there for one split second. We have to live here."

"NO!" screams Eve. "I can't bear it! I'll start thinking those fragments are the truth, are all there is, those little bits of white string! I refuse. I won't go back. I'll start believing in words again." She goes over to the bookcase and grabs book after book and hurls it against the wall. "That's all I'll have. I won't have real experiences, I'll just have fragments...fragments and the words...the words and...glimpses of the truth." She flops back down on the couch. "I don't even know what I'm talking about now...wait...I have to remember. I have to hold on to this. Clare! It's slipping away! Everything is slipping away. Wait!...there are no divisions...like...wait...like life and death...they're the same thing...Shit, now I'm just guessing again, suspecting, but back there I *knew*."

She sits on the couch with her arms covering her head, eyes closed, silent for a few minutes. "Oh my God. Everything's going to be exactly the same in the First Pearl when I get back, exactly the same as when I left it. Is it true, Clare? Will everything be exactly the same? What about Everything? Is it gone? Is everything the same there where you are as when I left?" Clare nods.

Eve gradually begins to notice, for the first time all night, that her body aches and her eyes are almost swollen shut. She can barely move. She bends stiffly down to the floor and picks up the washcloth. "This poor little washcloth," she says, laying it out across her knees, smoothing it flat. "This poor, finite, sweet little washcloth."

Eve looks out the window and sees that the sky is beginning to grow light. She hears birds chirping outside. "Little chirping birds," she says, weakly. "I must be back already."

Chapter Four

For the next few days, everything looks fragile to Eve, every object about to shatter into hundreds of sharp-edged pieces, to crack open and spill, to crash and burst into flame. She can't stand looking into the faces of people on the street, sees every line of age around their lips and eyes, their twitches, their scars, their paper-thin coatings.

Clare stays with Eve for two days and then goes back to David's. Eve goes about her life quietly, relieved at not having to speak to anyone, now that Clare has left. She walks with great difficulty, her whole body sore as if she had the flu.

She stays at home now almost all the time, walking anxiously around the apartment, examining every single object carefully, trying to discern if things are different now that she's back. She picks up a salt shaker, then a toothbrush, an apple, turning them in her hands, pacing the apartment, trying to decide.

She can't bear the thought that everything is back to normal, that nothing at all has changed as a result of her walk out to the end of the Pearl String. She panics at the thought of being trapped back in the First Pearl. At moments, she thinks maybe things are different and then she feels a surge of hope. At other times, she thinks it is all just as it was before. Finally, desperate to know, she decides to make a test.

She plans the test as follows: she will bake an apple pie, following the instructions of the recipe with *absolute impeccability*, and if the apple pie turns out to be an apple pie, (nothing more, nothing less), then she will have proved that everything has, in fact, returned to normal. But, on the other hand, if the ingredients turn out to be something different, (say, for example, she were to open the oven door and find a hammer and nails filling the pan), she will know that things are not the same, that her walk on the Pearl String has made a difference.

She looks up a recipe in a cookbook, carefully makes a list of all the ingredients she will need, and goes to the grocery to buy them. She can feel her heart beating too quickly, so she focuses even more tenaciously on her cooking project. She lays all the ingredients out on the kitchen table and checks the recipe over and over to make sure she has everything she needs before she begins.

As she holds each apple and peels it, she is quite hopeful that things are not exactly as they were before. She thinks that maybe her fingers are holding the apple differently, more tenderly perhaps. She feels that possibly she is more aware of the apple, its rounded curves, its red-green color, the differences in texture between its peel, its flesh and core.

She carefully measures the flour, the salt, the sugar and the shortening, reading the instructions over and over as she goes. She must make sure that if the apple pie turns out not to be an apple pie, it will be for the *right reasons*, and not because she merely made some common human error in its preparation.

She flours the rolling pin and rolls the dough out from the center, careful to use light, brisk movements to ensure that the crust will turn out light and flaky. She lifts the dough into the pie plate and then delicately places the slices of apple in a spiral pattern inside. She finishes the pie slowly and deliberately, culminating her task by making a beautiful, fluted design in the dough around the edges.

She is pleased with her work, rereads the recipe to make absolutely sure she has not forgotten any step along the way, and then places the pie in the pre-heated oven.

She sets the timer and busies herself cleaning up the kitchen, trying to wait patiently to find out the results of her test. As she is washing the mixing bowl and measuring spoons, she is quietly praying that the pie will be *anything* but a pie.

She imagines the possibilities. If she has actually been transformed as much as she hopes by her spinning down The Pearl String,
she imagines she will be rewarded by opening the oven door to find
the glowing, sweating face of Mary, smiling up at her from the halo
of the pie plate. Other possibilities speed through her head: a plate of
birds, a plate of snow, a plate of pearls! She smells pie crust and
cooking apples, but she tries not to let this worry her.

At last the buzzer goes off, and she leaps into the air, pot holders
clenched in a death grip, and gingerly opens the oven door. Inside, is
the most golden, perfectly-cooked apple pie she has ever seen. She
shakily puts it down on the kitchen table. She begins to despair as she
stares at the pie in front of her. Tears well up in her eyes, drop onto the
fluted edge of the pie crust, from which steam rises. Her wrists go limp
and the pot holders flop down onto the table. She turns off the oven,
takes a last look at the pie, and walks sadly into the living room.

An hour later Clare arrives to say hello and finds Eve lying on the
living room couch with a pillow over her head.

"Are you awake?" she asks. Eve lifts the pillow from her head and
gets up.

"Come here," she says, taking Clare's hand and leading her into
the kitchen. She points to the pie on the table. The whole room smells
sweet.

"A pie? Did you bake this?" asks Clare, in delight.

"I'm afraid I did," says Eve.

"It smells great!" says Clare. "It's beautiful. How come you look so
sad?"

"Because it was a test," says Eve. "I wanted to see if anything had
really changed...after The Pearl String...if a pie would be a pie, just an
ordinary pie. "

Clare looks at Eve.

"Well, what did you expect?"

"I expected something different. But nothing's changed. You try a
piece. You test it."

"I'd love to," says Clare. She sits down at the table and cuts a large
piece of the pie for herself. The pie is still warm. Eve sits down at the

table, too, and watches Clare intently, waiting for the verdict. Clare takes her first bite, dropping a piece of the crust onto her sweater, picking it back up with a grin and tucking it between her lips. It tastes delicious, and she is forced to confess, although somewhat hesitantly, that it's a perfect pie.

Eve stares down at the kitchen table, her fists clenched, thinking.

"Maybe it's a false test," suggests Clare, cutting herself another sliver of the pie.

Eve reaches up and finds a string of pearls tight around her neck. She fingers each one slowly, drawing conclusions.

"You take the pie home to David," she says. "I can't eat it."

Chapter Five

Later that evening, after Clare has left with the pie to go back to David's, Eve suddenly decides to go out for a walk. She hasn't been out for three days and doesn't realize there is a winter storm brewing. On her way out the door, she turns back, goes into her room, and gets her old copy of *The Republic* and brings it along. She winds through the Village streets, heading slowly downtown. An hour later, she finds herself beginning to cross the Brooklyn Bridge, the wind howling and screaming around her, the storm about to break loose.

Her feet are frozen, bare in her wet shoes, and she thinks of turning back, but she goes on. Now she regrets bringing *The Republic*—it's so heavy for her to carry, a leather-bound copy her father had given her years ago for her graduation from college. She thinks of tossing it into the water, but her father's own handwriting is in it, inscribed in the front. She stops for a moment on the bridge, in the fierce wind, opens the book, and reads the inscription:

> For my first-born, on her graduation
> from college. I am very proud of you
> and I know your mother would have
> been proud too.
>
> With all my love,
> Dad

She couldn't possibly get his dear handwriting wet. Maybe she could just tear out that page to save and toss the rest of the book into the water. But he gave her that book; she can't throw it away.

As she approaches the center of the bridge, the wind is so strong she has trouble moving forward. She pulls her raincoat tight around her, but it keeps blowing open, its buttons long gone. She is sweating under the raincoat, but shivering too. A man walking a few feet behind her is staring at her legs, bare, perfectly-shaven legs, uncovered in the middle of December. He notices how firm her calves are, how tight she holds them, how stiffly she walks. He finds her attractive and speeds up to talk to her. When he gets beside her, they are almost at the center of the bridge. He calls out something to her, but the wind and the traffic are so loud, she can't hear him. She doesn't want to talk to him, so she turns away from him and stops by the edge of the bridge, hoping he will pass. He slows down, stops for a second beside her, but he's too cold and he hurries on.

She is alone on the bridge now, looking down into the water. Her head starts spinning. She opens *The Republic*, hoping to stop the spinning by reading a page or two, but the words are blurry. She makes tiny pinches in her cheeks and eyelids with her fingernails. She pinches so hard, she leaves little red moons on both cheeks. But the spinning in her head increases with the howling of the wind. The sky darkens and it begins to snow.

As she falls from the bridge, the wind swirls up and catches her in its spin. Her raincoat flies open and catches on one arm, billowing out like a spinnaker, twirling her through the air. In one hand, she still holds *The Republic*. About halfway down to the water, the book is torn from her hand by the wind, and it falls through the air beside her, caught in the same spinning whirl of wind and snow. Just before she hits the water, her body is caught by a sudden updraft, which flips her over, and she hits head first.

Clare looks out the window of David's apartment just then and is happy to see that it has begun to snow. She wonders, for a moment, what Eve is doing tonight. Then she hears the tea kettle whistle, and runs to turn it off. She pours the steaming hot water over some chamomile leaves, and takes the pot of tea over to the table by the fireplace. She cuts two, big pieces of Eve's pie and she and David eat first one piece, and then, because it is so delicious, another and another, until the pie is all gone.

RECENT TITLES FROM FC2

From the District File
A novel by Kenneth Bernard
From the District File depicts a bureaucratic world of supercontrolled oppressiveness in the not-too-distant future. *Publishers Weekly* calls Bernard's fiction "a confrontation with the inexpressible...a provocative comment on the restrictiveness and pretension of our lives."
128 pages, Cloth: $18.95, Paper: $8.95

Double or Nothing
A novel by Raymond Federman
"Invention of this quality ranks the book among the fictional master-pieces of our age...I have read *Double or Nothing* several times and am not finished with it yet, for it is filled with the kinds of allusion and complexity that scholars will feast upon for years. Were literature a stock market, I'd invest in this book—Richard Kostelanetz
320 pages, Paper: $10.95

F/32
A novel by Eurudice
F/32 is a wild, eccentric, Rabaelaisian romp through most forms of amorous excess. But, it is also a troubling tale orbiting around a public sexual assault on the streets of Manhattan. Between the poles of desire and butchery, the novel and Ela sail, the awed reader going along for one of the most dazzling rides in recent American fiction.
250 pages, Cloth: $18.95, Paper, $8.95

Trigger Dance
Stories by Diane Glancy
"Diane Glancy writes with poetic knowledge of Native Americans...The characters of *Trigger Dance* do an intricate dance that forms wonderful new story patterns. With musical language, Diane Glancy teaches us to hear ancient American refrains amidst familiar American sounds. A beautiful book."—Maxine Hong Kingston
250 pages, Cloth: $18.95, Paper: $8.95

Is It Sexual Harassment Yet?
Stories by Cris Mazza
"The stories...continually surprise, delight, disturb, and amuse. Mazza's 'realism' captures the eerie surrealism of violence and repressed sexuality in her characters' lives."—Larry McCaffery
150 pages, Cloth: $18.95, Paper: 8.95

Napoleon's Mare
A novella by Lou Robinson
Napoleon's Mare, thirteen chapters and a section of prose poems is a diatribe, a discontinuous narrative—as much about writing as about the bewildering process of constructing a self.
186 pages, Cloth: $18.95, Paper: $8.95

Valentino's Hair
A novel by Yvonne Sapia
"Intense and magical, *Valentino's Hair* vividly creates an America intoxicated by love and death. Sapia brilliantly renders the vitality and tensions in the Puerto Rican community in 1920s New York City."—Jerome Stern. Picked as one of the top 25 books for 1991 by *Publishers Weekly*.
162 pages, Cloth: $18.95, Paper: $8.95

Mermaids for Attila
Stories by Jacques Servin
Mermaids for Attila is a fun, hands-on, toy-like book on the subject of well-orchestrated national behaviors. In it Servin considers the biggest horrors and the weirdest political truths. "At a time when conventional narrative fiction is making an utterly boring comeback, it is a relief to find writers like Jacques Servin who are willing to acknowledge that verbal representation can no longer be regarded as anything more than a point of departure."—Stephen-Paul Martin
128 pages, Cloth: $18.95, Paper: $8.95

Hearsay
A novel by Peter Spielberg
Hearsay is a darkly comic account of the misadventures of one Lemuel Grosz from youthbed to deathbed. In its blending of reality and irreality, *Hearsay* present a life the way we winess the life of another: from a certain distance, catching a glimpse here, a revelation there.
275 pages, Cloth: $18.95, Paper: $8.95

Close Your Eyes and Think of Dublin: Portrait of a Girl
A novel by Kathryn Thompson
A brilliant Joycean hallucination of a book in which the richness of Leopold Bloom's inner life is found in a young American girl experiencing most of the things that vexed James Joyce: sex, church, and oppression.
197 pages, Cloth: $18.95, Paper: $8.95

Books may be ordered through the Talman Company, 150 Fifth Avenue, New York, NY 10011.

For a catalog listing all books published by Fiction Collective, write to Fiction Collective Two, Department of English, Illinois State University, Normal, IL 61761-6901.